HELICOPTER

HARRY

Helicopter Harry
Summary:
[1. Fiction 2. Fantasy 3. Science fiction]

Imagine your ambitious dreams becoming a reality when you have a chance encounter with an indestructible helicopter pilot.

First Edition

Contents

THE COPTER KIDS

*Life is a magical opportunity, but you
have to create the magic!*

Kate and Kyle were sitting at the breakfast table staring at their cereal bowls when Mom asked, "Have you kids given any thought to what we discussed at dinner last night? How we thought it would be fun for you to spend some time at my law office so I can show you what I do. And you can spend a day with Dad at his office and see what engineering projects he is working on."

"Yes, I remember. But to be honest, Mom," Kate said, "they sound boring and our science teacher got us excited about aviation and becoming helicopter pilots. We studied everything that flies: from planes to helicopters to rocket ships. We read about Leonardo da Vinci and he got me excited with his hang glider and helicopter. A few weeks ago the Coast Guard landed their helicopter in the school football field and that was so exciting!"

"That's great," Mom said.

"It was so much fun," Kate continued. "We watched as it glided in and landed and I thought how magical that was. And the whole school got to climb into the helicopter, and sit in the pilot seats and play with the controls. Sitting in that big seat with my hands on the controls felt like I was in another world. That really sold me on being a pilot. Oh my god, I want to fly so badly, Mom. I closed my eyes when I was at the controls and imagined flying like a bird."

"I never thought you had such an interest in aviation. And I didn't know the Coast Guard had come to your school. That must have been so exciting for you both. We can always chat about it when you are older if it still interests you. Aviation is a man's job. Being an attorney is probably a better choice for you. And your father won't be happy since he loves his work and thinks Kyle will make a wonderful engineer like himself."

"Sure, Mom," Kate hesitated. "I know, but I'm a tomboy and like getting muddy. I'm more into guy things and I don't like dolls. And being an attorney sounds so girly."

"Hmm." Mom, stared. "Do you think you want to be a pilot like your sister?"

"Yes, and I can't wait. I know you and Dad will be upset, but I'm really excited about helicopters. And our science teacher said helicopter pilots are looked on as superheroes, since they save people's lives."

"Okay, then. Do you have capes?" Mom joked.

"No. But we are working on it! You can start sewing them," Kate joked.

Mom laughed. "You might need something to fall back on if your superhero gig doesn't work out." She smirked. "And you may see more opportunity and money as an attorney or engineer. Let's talk more about this later. What are your plans today?"

"We're going to Paradise Park to play with the remote control helicopters you got us," Kate said.

Mom thought to herself. *Oh yeah, I sort of planted that seed.* "Okay, that sounds like fun. Would you like a ride?" Mom asked.

"No, we'll ride our bikes," Kyle said.

"You be careful not to cause any trouble. Don't talk to any strangers and stay at the park so we know where you are."

"Yeah okay, Mom," Kate said.

As Kate and Kyle played with their helicopters at the park, they noticed that not many kids were there. Kate and Kyle were excitedly chasing each others helicopters when two older kids came out from behind some trees. The boy and girl were about thirteen years old. Both were wearing purple baseball caps turned backward, purple tennis shoes, white T-shirts, blue jeans and dark sunglasses. They had the letters "AS" circled on their shirts. "What are you kids doing in our park?" the boy demanded.

"It's not your park. We're just playing with our remote helicopters, so leave us alone!" Kate said sternly.

"Yes, *it i–'s* our park, and you need our permission to be here." The boy punched Kyle in the eye and Kyle fell to the ground. The boy then stepped on Kyle's helicopter, and the sound of crunching plastic echoed in the abrupt silence.

"Stay down, kid!" The boy shouted.

"Hey, leave my brother alone!" Kate cried. "And you're going to pay for that broken helicopter!"

"Make us, punk!" the girl said.

Kate gently pulled Kyle up and saw a red patch forming around his eye. A flash of pure anger swept through her. "Come on, Kyle. Let's fight these bullies!" she said.

"Not so fast, kid," the girl said. "Don't ever come back here or I will totally beat you up!" She stamped on Kate's helicopter and threw a punch at Kate's face, right in her eye. Kate landed on the ground beside her ruined helicopter.

Kate wiped away a tear and bounced up. "Hey, you bully, let's do this!!"

They were ready to fight when thunder roared in their ears and made their heads vibrate. The teenagers ran off at the sound of the approaching chopper "Watch out!" Kate yelled. "It's headed straight for us. Hurry! Grab your helicopter." She scooped up her mangled copter and dragged her brother away. Kate and Kyle ran as fast as they could through the park as a large red and black Huey helicopter streaked by. Then it circled back and hovered over them. Looking up at it, they tripped over each other's feet and then fell on top of each other.

"Get off me, Kyle!" Kate shouted.

The chopper was fifty feet above them, and the wind generated by the rotor blades made it difficult for them to stand up. The chaotic atmosphere also made it hard for them to hear each other. Then a voice came over the loudspeaker. "Are you okay?"

They could not understand what the pilot had said as it was so noisy. "Maybe it's the police coming to get you," Kate yelled. She huddled next to Kyle, both of them looking up at the red belly of the chopper that appeared to be closing in on them.

"More like, they're after those bullies!" Kyle yelled back.

Although Kate and Kyle were twins, Kate usually took the risk whenever adventure appeared. They were both dressed for a warm, sunny day with shorts, T-shirts and tennis shoes. As excited as they were about helicopters, they could never have imagined what this day had in store for them.

Suddenly there was a loud bang as flames and smoke exploded out of the engine-compartment door, blowing it clean off. Kate and Kyle watched in horror as the door sailed past them and stuck into the ground like a giant knife. The chopper wobbled back and forth as it attempted to land nearby, white and black smoke trailing behind it. The air smelled chokingly bitter from burning fuel. Smoke surrounded Kate and her brother.

As the chaos began to subside, Kate shouted, "Let's follow it!"

Kate and Kyle raced through the park and down a narrow alley. A fence loomed in front of them.

"That must be where the chopper was supposed to land!" Kyle said worriedly.

He and his twin sister clung to the fence like monkeys, their fingers sticking through the chain link. A no trespassing sign dangled underneath the rusty barbed wire that stretched along the top of the fence. The doomed helicopter was diving to the ground just beyond them. Smoke was pouring out of the cockpit, and flames billowed from the engine compartment. The heliport consisted of three tan warehouses and a couple of stationary helicopters. The windsock was made of underpants that were inflated by a slight breeze. The fence stretched as far as the eye could see.

"It's out of control!" Kate cried. "What can we do?"

Kyle had no time to answer. The chopper crashed just inside the heliport and burst into flames.

"Oh no. What about the pilot!" Kate yelled.

Just then, the pilot kicked the crumpled windshield out of the burning chopper. He rolled onto the tarmac, extinguishing the flames covering his clothes. He stood up just as flames engulfed the copter. The burning metal crackled and shot sparks into the air. Noticing Kate and Kyle, the pilot stared at them over his aviator glasses, pushing them up his nose as he headed toward them. Smoke trailed from his clothes.

"Whoa –" Kyle murmured.

The pilot was a long-legged, chiseled guy with wide shoulders. His baseball cap was tilted to keep the hot sun off his stubbly face. His blue jeans and flight jacket were charred and his skin was covered in black soot. As he neared the fence, the air became heavy with the pungent smell of jet fuel and burned wreckage.

"Looks like it's toast, mister," Kyle said.

"That's not the best way to land a helicopter!" the pilot said, shaking his head. Then he grimaced. "Now it's a million-dollar piece of rubbish, unless it undergoes major reconstruction."

He paused, "What are you kids doing here?" he asked.

"Uh...we were getting bullied by a couple of kids in the park when you flew over us. They ran off, but we followed you. We want to be helicopter pilots like you," Kyle said with shining eyes. "Can you teach us about helicopters?"

"So they gave you both black eyes?" The pilot shook his head. "I wasn't sure if you were in trouble but it looked like those kids were bothering you."

"Yeah, they punched us, but we couldn't hear you over the noise. But we were ready to fight when you buzzed over us."

"Do you want some ice for those black—and—blue eyes?"

"No. They don't hurt. Do they Kyle?" Kate said.

"No, not really," Kyle said.

"I see they destroyed your toy helicopters. Toss them in the trash and I'll get you new ones."

"That is nice of you, mister," Kate said, "but Mom said not to accept gifts from strangers."

"That's very good advice, no new helicopters, then! And I hate bullies. Sorry I didn't fly over sooner."

"Helicopters are very cool, and I'm glad you're a fan like I was at your age."

The twins sighed, and they let go of the fence. The chopper let out another loud explosion, as if to say its final goodbye. Kate looked back. "How did you survive a fiery crash like that, mister? Most people would have died…unless you're some kind of superhero."

"It's more about knowing your ABCs," said the mysterious man, with a dimpled smile.

"We know our ABCs!" Kate fired back.

"Not the ones that count," he said.

"Look, mister, we're on a mission, to learn more about helicopters," Kate said. "That's why we've been hanging around near the heliport. Our science teacher recently taught our class about the magical world of helicopters and how it's a miracle they can even fly. He even told us about a legendary helicopter that the public has been forbidden to see. They say it can fly like no other helicopter on earth."

The pilot shrugged. "I have no idea what you're talking about, kid. And you're not supposed to be here," he said crossly. "Helicopters are for grown-ups, not kids."

"Are we in trouble?" Kyle asked. Are we going to be arrested?"

"Maybe," the pilot told him. "You *are* trespassing."

"Hey, you have a British accent. Are you a secret agent?" Kate asked excitedly.

The pilot smirked. "Bond, James Bond!"

"Nice try, mister," Kate said.

"Now, as you can see, I'm pretty busy at the moment. You kids aren't in trouble, but it's time to go home and have your eyes looked at."

Kate put her arm around her brother's shoulders and they began to walk away with their heads down. As if it wasn't enough for them to get bullied, then rejected by the mysterious pilot!

He watched as they walked away. "Okay, wait!" the pilot called out. "I love your enthusiasm for helicopters. Do you two live around here?"

"About a mile away," Kyle said, turning around. "Our parents don't want us to become pilots. They told us it's too dangerous, so we should quit dreaming. They said we should keep our heads out of the clouds and stay focused on school."

"I see. That's a shame." The pilot gazed at some white puffy clouds and then returned his gaze to them.

"You do need to focus on school, but you also need to follow and nurture your dreams." He suddenly looked worried. "Do your parents know where you are?"

"Yeah," Kyle said. "They think were playing in the park with our toy helicopters."

"What do you say we give them a call? I'll pretend to be James Bond."

"No. You can't do that!" Kate pleaded. "We'll get in big trouble if they find out we were talking to a stranger, let alone an indestructible pilot."

"Mom warned us not to talk to strangers in the park. Now we are in trouble," Kyle said.

The pilot hesitated, looked at his watch, and said, "Well...I'll show you a few things, but then you need to be on your way so your parents won't worry."

"Woo-hoo!" the twins cried with excitement.

The pilot walked up to an eye scanner on the gate. The scanner had flashing red lights that turned green as he pushed it. He moved his sunglasses up to his forehead and looked into it. The latch clicked as he pulled the black metal gate toward him. He slid his glasses back down and held the gate open just wide enough so the children could slide through. The gate slammed behind them with a loud clang. It locked and the lights turned red again.

"This gate is pretty secure. Can't have any brats sneaking in here to check out the choppers," he said.

"We're not brats!" Kate said.

He chuckled. "Sorry, I meant 'kids.' A lot of kids come snooping around here." He extended his hand to shake Kate's.

"I'm Helicopter Harry."

"I'm Kate, and this is my twin brother Kyle. Why did you circle around us in the park?"

"I got a call from some parents to search for some lost children. Are you lost?"

"Of course not," Kate said. "Although that would be something my mom might do." She rolled her eyes and smiled, poking Kyle.

"But you're not lost, right? Could it have been your mom calling me out on a search?"

"No, no, it's fine," Kate said with a smile. "We aren't expected back till later. That must be other kids who got lost. Don't you have to get back to searching for them? Or call to say your helicopter blew up?"

"I detect an attitude about your parents," Harry said.

"Yeah," Kate said with a sigh, "we love them, but they hover over us all the time. They always think they know what's best. Why can't they give us some space and let us follow our dreams? They must have had dreams once too. What happened?"

Harry gave her a gentle smile. "Maybe they're jealous of your dreams to be pilots because they do jobs they find boring."

"Oh, that's deep, dude," Kate said, laughing.

"What's Kate short for? Katrina? Katherine? Or just Katie?"

"If you must know, it's short for Katherine, but please just call me Kate."

"Careful, Harry. She's a feisty one," Kyle said, grinning mischievously.

Harry chuckled. "Quite right! Tell me about yourself, then. I don't see many girls sneaking around here who want to be pilots."

"Kate's a tomboy and adventurous. She hangs out with my friends more than hers," Kyle said.

"Oh yeah, I like video games," Kate chimed in. "And my brother is a book nerd. He doesn't watch TV and just reads book after book. But he plays video games with me."

"I see. What do you like to read about, Kyle?" Harry asked.

"Well, I've read a lot of books on aviation. But I like to read science fictio too."

A dragonfly with rainbow-colored wings landed on Harry's shoulder.

"That's the largest and prettiest dragonfly I've ever seen," Kate said.

"He's as tough as they come for an old fossil. Isn't that right, Machismo?" Harry said.

"Pretty funny, dude," Machismo said. "Maybe that's because I'm the closest thing there is to a prehistoric helicopter." He turned to the twins and continued. "I'm a relative of the giant helicopter dragonfly from South America, the birthplace of dinosaurs." Machismo stood up on his hind legs, puffed out his yellow chest, and pounded on it with his feet.

"What the...?" Kyle said, his eyes wide. "Machismo can talk?

"Yep, all the animals and helicopters here speak, which is part of the android magic of this place," Harry said, gestureing in the distance as he circled around, pointing his finger towards the vast area surrounded by a chain-link fence.

"What's android magic?" Kate asked.

"Well, it's man and machine. The people here in the special place are not real people but cyborgs. And the animals here are not real animals but androids. After the real animals died out, they were rebuilt as robots—but robots that can speak and fly," Harry said.

"So this is, like, a mythical world?" Kyle said.

Harry smiled. "Oh yes, Kyle. It's like nothing else you'll ever experience in your lifetime. I've spent years working with cutting-edge technology to bring these beautiful creatures and machines back to life."

"Oh, you're a scientist like Doctor Frankenstein?"

"Scientist yes, mad no. The technology is beyond belief. The choppers can morph from animal to helicopter. I know it sounds like a fantasy, but it's quite real. The helicopters can fly themselves but I like to fly them too."

The children stared at Harry, unable to believe what they were hearing. Kyle whispered to Kate, "This is creepy. Maybe we should go home."

"Oh stop it, silly," Kate said. "It's just a fun adventure. You'll see!"

"Um—okay. This is a lot to take in Harry. How did you get the name Helicopter Harry?" asked Kyle. "Seems like an odd name."

Harry removed his soot-covered sunglasses, revealing a pair of piercing green eyes. "Well, my parents didn't support my dream of becoming a pilot either. So when I turned eighteen, I left home and joined the military to make my dream come true. But before I share any more about myself, I must advise you that my life is top secret. You both must swear that you'll never reveal this information to anyone."

Nervously, Kate replied, "Of course, Harry. I swear."

"Me too, Harry," Kyle said. "I'll never tell a single soul."

Harry extended his hand, and Kate and Kyle reached out and shook it.

"I was assigned to a test project called Whirly Wings," Harry said. "I had a real copter pack attached to my back. It was the coolest thing ever. I wore a motor on my back and had a propeller extending above my head. I know it sounds funny, but I actually flew, which was incredi–bly exciting. I flew secret missions behind hostile terri—tory, searching for troublemakers. Unfortunately, I had a bad accident one day. Some of the troublemak-ers heard me flying back to base and began to shoot at me. I was two-hundred feet off the ground when bullets pinged off my silver motor casing. The copter pack was supposed to be bulletproof, but a bullet pierced the motor casing. The motor exploded and disengaged the rotor sending the motor to the ground. The next thing I knew, I was spinning out of control upside down when I hit the ground."

"I bet that hurt," Kyle said.

"Yes, and the propeller went through my back and came out between my lungs with my heart skewered on the end. When I hit the ground, I died."

"Oh my god, you died!" Kyle, said, chuckling under his breath. "You're pulling our legs. Your heart was skewerded?"

"Really? You died?" Kate said, laughing.

"I was dead alright! But I had an operation that brought me back to life as a cyborg."

The twins had slack jaws.

"Luckily, I was found in time and rushed to the cyborg chamber. Special top-secret technicians inserted subder-mal titanium body armor under my skin. It makes me bulletproof while rebuilding my mangled body with new smart-brain technology that's controlled by my smart watch and phone. I can make my hands turn into rotors that enable me to fly. I am more machine than human— now, " Harry said.

"Wow, not human but machine?" Kyle repeated.

"Yes, but I still have many human characteristics. Like my skin and body. I still look human but I now have a motherboard for a brain which is programmed to the smallest detail of being a human."

"Whoa, that's so cool!" Kyle said.

Harry demonstrated his hand rotors. He stretched his arms, interlaced his fingers and cracked his knuckles. This disengaged his fingers as silver hand rotors popped out. Harry activated the rotors and controlled the speed with his thoughts as he lifted off.

Kate and Kyle giggled and couldn't believe their eyes, as Harry hovered over them for a minute and then landed. "Can we have hand rotors too?" Kate asked.

"Maybe someday when you become cyborgs," Harry joked.

"Wow, Harry. Maybe we could ride on your back and fly over to our school. We could dive-bomb the school yard at lunchtime and scare the kids," Kate said.

"That would be fun alright, but maybe another time," Harry said with a laugh.

"And then what happened?" Kyle asked.

"My friends nicknamed me Helicopter Harry. And I flew a few more missions behind enemy lines to eliminate bullies."

"You're a superhero!" Kate said.

"Sure, you could say that. Yeah, a superhero," Harry said.

"Who were the people you were fighting?" Kyle asked.

"They are hostile people, and they have become bullies, which come in all sizes and ages. I'm sure you have playground bullies at your school like the kids from the park."

"Oh, yes. They are always picking on us at school and giving us wedgies. They say bad things on social media about us being twins and short," Kate said.

"So," Kyle looked at the ground. "How old do we have to be to learn to fly?" he asked.

"How old are you right now?" Harry asked.

"We're ten years old," Kate said.

"Then ten it is! As long as you believe in yourself and have a limitless imagination, you're already a sort of a superhero. How much do you two know about helicopters?"

"We know they're really cool," Kyle said.

"And they can fly fast," Kate said. "Oh, and this old guy named da Vinci sorta created one five-hundred years ago but it never flew. We learned that in science class."

Machismo darted over Kate and Kyle.

"Here comes more of my team," Harry said excitedly. "I'm sure you'll both want to meet them. Billy Bob the bumblebee and Chantal the hummingbird!"

"Did you rebuild them into androids as well?"

"You bet, but some of them have a screw loose, like our class clown, Billy Bob."

"We all know da Vinci dreamed larger than life and had his head in the clouds like the rest of you knuckleheads!" Billy Bob shouted. He laughed as he buzzed around everyone's faces. Billy Bob was a country bumpkin with a small black head and big blue eyes. His yellow belly was so big that he almost tripped over it. "Helicopters are just glorified android robots anyway," the plump little bee said with a laugh.

"Oh, what a cute hummingbird and bee," Kate said.

"Mom loves her hummingbird feeders and collects bee honey from the neighbors' bee hives," Kyle said.

"How nice, kids. I'm always looking for new feeders to raid. Is your place close by?" Chantal said.

"About a mile. It's the dark red house on Pine Cone Drive," Kate said. "You can't miss it."

"Perfect, thank you."

"Sure, but leave my honey hives alone, kid," Billy Bob said.

"Kids, don't pay any attention to Billy Bob. He's just jealous because there aren't any choppers designed after him." Billy Bob darted around everyone, stopped and bowed. Chantal strutted around, preening her blue-green feathers and pointing her long, pointy beak in the air.

"Yeah, yeah, yeah, like we care about old farts, smarty-pants," Billy Bob said. "Jealousy has nothing to do with it, although your beady black eyes do have a way of penetrating right through me."

"We did find it interesting that we celebrate the same birthday as da Vinci, and that he was left-handed like us," Kate said. "When is your birthday, Harry, and how old are you?" she asked.

"Well, I'm older than you, but not as old as the King of England. How's that?"

Kate giggled.

"Do you know how da Vinci came up with the idea of the helicopter?" Harry asked the twins.

Kyle shrugged. "Not really."

Kyle and Kate leaned in closer, almost touching noses with the mysterious Harry.

"We love reading about da Vinci and his inventions. He was way ahead of his time," Kate said.

"Yeah, everyone in the class loved it when we studied his art and cool inventions," Kyle said.

"So, who's the fastest?" Kate asked.

Machismo flapped his fluorescent wings. "Dragon-flies, of course! We're the closest thing to a real helicopter, because our wings act almost like a chopper's rotor. They flap 100 times per second, and I can fly at 60 miles per hour. I'm the world's fastest, stealthiest insect." He zipped forward and back a few times, before coming to an immediate stop above everyone. He then bowed, wrapping himself in his wings like a cloak.

Everyone laughed.

"You know," Chantal said, "leave it to an old fossil and a bumblebee to brag about being the best, but when it comes to wing speed, I win. My wings can flap 200 times a second." She flapped her wings; zoomed up, down, and around; and whizzed by upside down near the twins' faces. "What's more, I can fly 50 miles an hour while upside down. I also get power from my wings when they come up, not just when they go down like most other birds. This allows me to hover like no other."

"Excuse me!" Billy Bob shouted. "The great pollinator has something to say. Although my wing-flap speed is 160 times a second, it's still faster than any pesky dragonfly." He fluttered his wings, sputtering as fast as he could.

"And if it weren't for me and my friends pollinating every plant in sight, you might not have anything to eat." Billy Bob landed on Harry's right shoulder, leaned back, and pushed out his big belly.

"Oh my god, maybe back off the honey and start flapping your wings faster," Chantal said.

"And if your wings didn't flap 200 times a second, you would never get your pudgy flight-challenged body off the ground," Machismo scoffed."

"And besides, how fast can you fly?" Chantal said.

"On a good day, with a wind at my back, 30 miles an hour." Billy Bob stuck out his tongue at her and made a fart sound.

The twins laughed.

"I rest my case," Chantal said. "And it's a miracle of science that you can even fly." She turned to the children. "Billy Bob fell on his head during one of his historic flights, in case you were thinking he's a little slow."

Everyone except Billy Bob laughed.

"I dream about the time when dragonflies roamed the earth with the dinosaurs and were larger than life," Machismo reminisced. "Back then we had a wingspan of three feet."

Billy Bob laughed. "Hey, Grandpa, why don't you fly back to your rest home and reminisce with your dinosaur friends?"

Hearing the flapping of wings, Kyle looked up and saw a pterodactyl circling overhead. "Who's that up there?" he asked, not believing his eyes.

Kate looked up as well. "What the, a dinosaur? This keeps getting better and better."

"Oh," Chantal said. "That's the patriarch of the neighborhood. At least, that's what he thinks."

Brutus the pterodactyl appeared as a wizardly sorcerer from out of a white cloud. He swooped in and landed on a grassy area and slid to a stop. He had a muscly body and a commanding head. He had long sharp teeth that protruded from his jaws when his was mouth closed. His leathery skin stretched over his body, and his massive wings spanned twelve feet.

"Oh, great," Chantal remarked, as she touched wing tips with Brutus. "Now ya did it, big bad Brutus. You're just another show-off, always wanting to strut your stuff."

"Thanks, Chantal, for the introduction," Brutus said. "But you're just a bunch of amateurs. Who cares about wing speed? Let's cut to the chase. I have millions of years of experience, and I'm not even going to brag about my wing speed, since I could flap you all back into history. Da Vinci was a bright guy—I could tell you stories about him and his inventions until you all died from boredom!" Brutus looked at the twins, paused, and laughed, as did the twins. "But you two aren't here for that."

Kyle beamed. "You're right, but we think pterodactyls are the coolest dinosaur ever!"

"Why, thank you, son. Carry on, Harry."

"Brutus and I have things in common when it comes to taking out bad people. Brutus has a special interest in bullies and likes to eat them."

"Really? Kate asked.

"Oh yes, and the bigger the better."

"Do you eat children?" Kyle asked.

"Only if they are bullies."

"Maybe you could stop by our school sometime," Kate said.

"We know some kids you could eat right now!" Kyle said.

"The ones that gave you black and blue eyes, I'm assuming," Brutus said.

"Yes, can you please!" Kate said.

"Well, I have to find them first," he said.

"They were at the park and wore purple baseball caps and purple tennis shoes," Kyle said.

"I'll go take a look, and see what I can find," he said and flew off.

Harry paused and looked Kate and Kyle up and down. Okay, I showed you a few things, but shouldn't you go show your parents your black eyes now? Won't they be worried?"

"We've had black eyes before from school bullies because we're so small for our age. And it's still early in the day, so they won't be worried. Can you please teach us to be superheroes?" Kate asked.

"Um...well," Harry hesitated and scratched his chin.

"Okay. Let me tell you something. And again, you can't reveal what I'm going to tell you."

"Okay, Harry. We promise," Kate said with a big smile.

"I have a superhero bootcamp here, where I teach kids who have unique qualities to become superheroes."

"A bootcamp? You had us fooled!" Kyle said, giving his sister a fist bump.

"And what is the purpose of your bootcamp?" Kate asked.

"I need help to fight Will, who is the leader of the Kommando Kids, which is a group of school bullies. Maybe we should call and ask your parents if this is okay, since it will take all day."

"Like I said, they will say no and tell us to come home right away," Kate said. "But I will send them a text and tell them we will be at the park all day. Okay I sent it."

Kate's phone dinged with an incoming text. "They said okay," Kate said.

"Alright, then." Harry hesitated again. "If you think you are ready. There are eleven stages to this bootcamp, and you will be tested mentally and physically through each one. The people and machines you meet along the way will be evaluating you. They are all cyborgs and androids. If you do make it to the end, you will be rewarded with your own superhero powers and a tattoo that represents a true superhero. There will be missteps along the way, and you might even die. But they are designed to make you stronger."

"Cool, a tattoo!" Kyle said.

"Yes, a tattoo on your inner wrist to show that you have conquered the challenge of bootcamp and not to mess with you."

"What does it look like?" Kate asked.

"I'll only show you if and when you succeed."

Kate looked at Kyle and said, "Let's do it!"

"Not so fast, sis, Harry said we might die. Maybe we should think about this, talk to Mom and Dad, and come back another day," Kyle said.

"I know it's scary, Kyle, but I have an idea. Let's flip a coin—heads, we stay or tails—we go home," Kate replied.

"Okay, go for it Kate," Kyle said with a concerned look on his face.

Kate pulled a shiny quarter from her pocket and flipped the coin. He caught it before it landed on the ground. Harry slowly opened his hand, with his and Kate's eyes locked onto his long fingers. Without blinking, he slowly unpeeled one finger and then another. The suspense built on the kids' faces as his last finger opened, "It's heads!"

"Woohoo," Kate screamed with excitement.

"So, we won't die, Harry?" Kyle asked.

"Sorry, I can't promise you, Kyle."

"Okay, let's do this!" Kate said. "We're fast learners, and we love hard work and near-death experiences. Don't we, Kyle?"

"Sure, Kate. And if we die, we come back as cyborgs, right Harry?" Kyle asked with anticipation.

Harry laughed. "Sure thing, Kyle," He winked at Kate.

"Okay then, but let's take a timeout so you catch your breath and grab a drink of water since we have a lot to go over." They all walked over to the water cooler and handed each of them a paper cup with water in it. They all sat down on a nearby bench.

"Thanks, Harry, we needed that. We are ready to get this party started," Kate said. "Isn't that right Kyle?"

"You bet, let's get to it!" Kyle said.

"Okay, let's start with the pilot's ABCs," Harry said. "*A* is for Attitude: always be positive. *B* is for Brave, like a superhero. *C* is for Cool. Yes, you want to look cool, but more importantly, you want to stay cool, calm, and collected in the face of danger!"

"What kind of danger?" Kyle asked.

"I'll be honest, flying helicopters can be dangerous. However, there's no danger in flying with the right attitude."

"Okay," Kate said, and fist-bumped Harry. Kyle also fist-bumped Harry.

"Follow my lead," Harry instructed as he stood and gestured for the twins to do the same. "As I close my eyes, close yours as well and visualize. Your brain is your strongest muscle, and the power to believe is in your mind. As you believe, so shall it be."

"Nothing's happening," Kate said after a few moments. "And this is a little scary. What are we doing? Is this safe?"

"It's okay to be a little worried; most youngsters are," Harry said. "Just relax and take a deep breath."

"Okay, Harry, I feel a little better," Kate said.

"You must activate your imagination, which is more powerful than any superhero power. Believe and declare you're superheroes, capable of anything you want to achieve in life! Each of you, take my hand and prepare to be empowered."

Harry's muscular hands enveloped the twins' hands and squeezed them tightly. His energy passed from his hands to theirs. The kids' faces lit up and they became energized.

"Now repeat after me," he said. "We believe. We believe we are superheroes."

The children looked at each other and chanted, "We belieeeeevvvvve! We belieeeeevvvvve!"

"I think something's happening," Kyle said.

"That means it's working," Harry said.

White T-shirts, blue jeans, and boots appeared on Kate and Kyle, followed by baseball caps and sunglasses. Finally, their tattered flight jackets appeared.

"Wow! Aren't these the coolest jackets, Kate? This is fantastic!" Kyle exclaimed. "Are we dreaming?" He stared directly into Kate's eyes through his new aviator glasses and turned his hat backward.

"Is this for real?" Kate asked. "Wow! I feel like I drank five energy drinks. Are we superheroes?"

"Not quite, but you are on your way," Harry said.

"Are we cyborgs?" Kate asked.

"Nope," Harry said.

"Then can I be a superhero princess?" Kate asked with a grin.

Harry raised an eyebrow. "Is there such a thing?"

"There is now," she said proudly.

"Okay. Princess. Your flight jackets will empower you, but without them, you'll just be ordinary children. So don't lose them."

"Oh my god! Check me out, Kyle. I'm a superhero pilot!" Kate said.

"Me too! These are the coolest jackets," Kyle said. "I totally feel like a superhero." In a British accent, he added, "Bond, James Bond."

Kate bent over, laughing. "Nice try, Kyle."

Machismo called out, "Harry, Chantal, Brutus, and you too, Billy Bob, come over here for a second."

They all gathered away from Kate and Kyle behind another helicopter, out of earshot.

"What is it with you and these brats, Harry?" Machismo said. "Kids come up to the gate all the time, and you almost always send them away..."

Harry stroked his chin. "I don't know, there's something different about these two. They have big imaginations and think anything is possible. They remind me of myself when I was their age."

"But we're all top-secret androids and can't be discovered," Machismo said, looking concerned.

"Oh, would you stop already?" Chantal said, shaking her head. "They're just little brats barely out of diapers. Until we know they're not spies, we have to treat them as such. Companies are starved for cutting-edge technology for their next chopper. Can you imagine if our smart technology got into the wrong hands? It would change the world—and not in a good way. I'll stay high and keep an eye on the twins. Brutus, give guidance as needed but don't eat them."

"Only if they are spies," Brutus said.

"Okay, deal. Billy Bob, just be the dumble dork you are, and try not to talk too much. I'll help Harry with the training."

As Kate and Kyle watched Harry and the gang talking, Kate nudged her brother. "Mom would freak if she saw us now."

Kyle laughed. "Oh yeah, superhero kids."

Machismo

You catch more flies with honey than with vinegar.

Harry said, "Tell me more about your parents. What do your parents do for a living?"

"Like we said, Harry," Kate began, "they're not really supportive, but we do love them as our parents."

"Mom is an attorney," she said, "and Dad is an engineer. They work downtown and are stuck in traffic for hours at a time. Sometimes They don't get home till after dark and past dinner time. Dad seems stressed most of the time. I don't think they like their jobs. I'll hear him pull into the garage at night. And he will slam his car door and speak to himself—*Not another day of this madness,* after he kicks or throws something. He then opens the door to the kitchen and says, —*"Hi honey, I'm home."* And he always asks the same thing—*"How was your day?"*— to everyone in a cheery voice. It's the same thing every day. We don't tell him we can hear him speak to himself." Kate said.

"Hm. Although those sound like frustrating professions, you'll make more money doing one of those than being a pilot or a superhero."

"Boringggg. Sitting in an office all day staring at a computer, stuck in traffic, and wanting to barf! Maybe that's good for them," Kyle said, "but not for us!"

"Okay, then. Simply put, the helicopter is a combination of animal and machine that vibrates around five quarts of oil—connected by a few rubber bands," explained Harry.

"Very funny," said Machismo who was sitting on Harry's shoulder. "But let's show them the chopper that was designed after me."

"Sure, let's see some magic!" Harry said. Machismo fluttered his wings, and then flew off Harry's shoulder. When he landed on the tarmac, he grew until he was several times the size of the children. The flutter of his wings made a vibration that sounded like a rotor blade spinning through the air: *WHOOSH.*

"Wow! That's so awesome, you are a magical one! You're big enough to ride, Machismo," Kyle said. "Can we go for a spin?"

Harry smiled. "Why not? It'll blow your minds."

Machismo smiled too. "Hop aboard, kids."

Kyle and Kate climbed onto Machismo's back, and then they took off and flew over the heliport. They flew up to five-hundred feet and could see their neighborhood beyond the park. A loud buzz came from Machismo's wings as they fluttered through the air. The children looked down and saw Harry waving at them. He appeared small, while the mountains loomed large in the distance.

"Hang on tight!" Harry shouted up to them.

"Oh man!" Kate yelled, as the wind blew in her face. "This is so much fun."

"Yeah, this is the best. Can it get any more fun?" Kyle said, catching his hat before it blew off his head.

"Yes, it can," Machismo said, gently landing back on the tarmac. "Climb off, and watch this."

The twins climbed off Machismo's back and then backed away as he transformed into a helicopter. They stared in awe as Machismo's blue, yellow, and red insect body cracked as he steadily increased in size, revealing a bright yellow and red helicopter fuselage.

His tail rotor popped out from the end of his body. Then, his rainbow-colored wings fluttered feverishly and dissolved into a large, shiny rotor that reflected the sun's rays as it slowly spun to a stop. Machismo's head morphed into the cockpit. His eyes were on either side of the bubble windshield, and his mouth was below the windshield.

"Go on, you two. Climb inside," Harry said.

Kate and Kyle climbed inside the cockpit, their mouths hanging open.

"How in the world did Machismo do that?" Kate asked.

"That's part of the magic of this place. Don't even try to question it," Harry said, "because it goes beyond the unbelievable."

Machismo spoke up.—"You'll refer to me as the Macho Machine from now on— the most magnificent helicopter ever!"

"Oh, stop, Machismo. You're far from the best, Maybe you are one of the strangest androids ever," Harry said with a laugh. He walked over to the helicopter and gave the glistening rotor a spin. "Kate, Kyle, this is the helicopter most kids learn to fly in. This big, honking shiny piece of metal is the rotor. It's like the wing of an airplane and spins incredibly fast to generate lift, just like on your toy helicopters."

"Let me give the lesson!" Machismo said, interrupting Harry.

"Be my guest, Machismo." Harry stepped back. "The stage is yours."

"How fast does your rotor spin?" Kyle asked.

"Its speed can get up to 400 miles an hour," Machismo responded, puffing with pride.

"Wow! That's fast!" Kate exclaimed. "Do you fly that fast?"

"No. As a helicopter, I can only fly about 150 miles an hour, and that depends on how much gas I have in the tank." Machismo said. "But I prefer to cruise at about 100 miles an hour."

The children laughed and stared at Machismo with enormous grins on their faces.

"Kyle, grab the cyclic stick located in front of you," Harry said. "It's also known as the joystick. It makes the helicopter fly forward and left and right. Move it around. Think about flying a helicopter like you'd drive a car. You have a key for the ignition, as well as a gas pedal and a steering wheel. It's that easy."

Kyle took a hold of the cyclic stick as Harry continued to guide him. "Yeah, Harry," he said, "we know a lot about driving a car. We snuck out with our mom's Camaro one night and crashed it into a telephone pole."

Kate rolled her eyes at Kyle and put her finger over her lips.

"Yeah, Kate, you crashed it into a telephone pole and blamed me since you knew how mad Mom and Dad would be!" Kyle said.

"Oh, you d-didn't!" Harry stuttered. "You two aren't such little angels after all—Maybe you're even a little wild." He shook his head. "What have I gotten myself into? Okay, by pushing forward or side to side on the cyclic, you can steer the helicopter like you would a car."

"Hey, don't push so hard on the stick," Machismo hollered. "It doesn't take much to steer me—just a touch."

"Sorry, Machismo," Kyle said. "It's just like the joystick on my video game."

"But unlike your video game," Machismo said, "the cyclic stick can take you places you've never dreamed of!"

"And this black bar is the collective," Harry said, pointing to the black bar next to the seat. "Go ahead. Grab it, Kate. By pulling up on the collective, you make the helicopter go up. By pushing down on it, you make the chopper go down. It's that simple. Now check out the gas pedal. It's a throttle grip, like a motorcycle has," Harry continued. "It's located at the end of the collective handle and gives gas to the chopper, just like you'd roll on the throttle with a motorcycle."

"This is very confusing Harry," Kate said.

VROOM! VROOM! Suddenly they all heard the sound of a motorcycle approaching.

"Speaking of motorcycles," Harry said, "that sounds like Carlita. Here she comes on her new, cool, torch-red sport bike."

Carlita pulled over, removed her red helmet, and shook back her long black hair. Her black leather jacket and pants, which fit her body like a glove, glistened in the sunlight as she got off her bike. "*Hello,* handsome," she said as she waltzed over to Harry. Harry grabbed her by the hand, spun her around, kissed her on the cheek, and then spun her back.

"Hello, sweetheart. I'm teaching Kyle and Kate about helicopters. Would you like to help? We were discussing the throttle."

The twins climbed out of the cockpit to greet Carlita.

"Cool bike, Carlita," Kyle said.

"Quite the greeting, Carlita," Kate said.

"Oh, it's nothing. It's how we greet each other all the time," Carlita said.

"She shook their hands and noticed Harry's still-smoldering chopper. "I see you've been practicing your crash landings again, Harry.

"Hey," Kyle said, "Do you work here?"

"You bet!" Carlita said, winking at Harry.

"Are you a cyborg like Harry?" Kate asked.

"Oh yeah," Carlita said. She looked at Harry, winked, again, and asked, "Shall we dance?" Both she and Harry engaged their hand rotors and zoomed around the heliport in unison. They stopped within a foot of each other in mid-air. They were twenty feet above the twins. They each turned one hand rotor off, embraced and took a few dance steps and then landed.

"Wow. You guys are so romantic!" Kate said.

"That was unreal!" Kyle said. "So how did you die and become a cyborg?"

"Harry and I were racing. I was driving my motorcycle and Harry was driving his new electric cybertruck down the freeway at 150 miles per hour on a beautiful, sunny crisp morning. I was pulling ahead of Harry and he was letting me win. I was pretty far ahead when out of nowhere a giant truck broadsided me, causing me to crash. I hit the pavement hard, and then the other driver turned around and ran over me. It was either Will or one of his gang—Will had recently been booted off the team for being a bully. He started out like you at ten years old. He was a good kid. But then his brother died and everything changed. He said he didn't like being treated as a toddler and ended up being kicked out of school and wouldn't listen to adults. And then he became a bully and terrorized younger kids. He was eventually run over by a group of kids that he bullied. We thought that was the end of it until he was rebuilt into a cyborg. Something went terribly wrong after the operation to rebuild him. He got the wrong chip or motherboard since Harry couldn't chase him like the others because he has superpowers that Harry can't match. I died shortly after Will ran me over and he needed to take me to his top-secret technicians. In two hours I was back in the saddle of my motorcycle with titanium under my skin. I was equipped with lasers, hand rotors and rocket launchers and I could fight like a ninja warrior. I could also ride my motorcycle and not worry about dying."

"Maybe he thinks you or Harry ran him over, and this is payback," Kyle said.

"Wow, that's a hard one to understand," Kate exclaimed.

"Hold on, you didn't tell me you have rocket launchers!" Harry said.

"Yes, I came with upgraded technology," Carlita answered.

"I see," Harry said. "I should be ready for an upgrade then."

"So far it's only for new cyborgs," Carlita said.

"Oh jeez," sighed Harry.

"That sounds like the kids that bullied us in the park," Kate said. "They had the symbol AS on their shirts. They were intent on hurting us until Harry swooped in with his chopper."

"Can we go for a ride on your motorcycle?" Kyle asked.

"Let's ask Harry," Carlita said.

"Sure, go ahead and scare them! Just kidding," Harry joked.

"Kyle, climb onto the motorcycle and give the throttle a twist."

Kyle watched excitedly as Carlita started the motorcycle. It crackled to a roar and sounded fast. He climbed onto the sport bike and straddled the seat in front of Carlita. *VROOM! VROOM!* As he twisted the throttle handle, he felt the vibration of the motor throughout his body. Harry handed him a helmet.

"Easy there," Carlita said. "Just a twist. It doesn't take much to make this baby fly."

"Incredible!" Kyle said. They spun around the heliport following the white line that guided the choppers in and out of hangars. They were back in a matter of seconds.

"My turn!" yelled Kate. She was as eager as Kyle, as neither of them had ever been on a motorcycle before. She climbed on, stretched herself out over the gas tank, and then twisted the throttle. Kyle handed her the helmet, and Kate put it on. *VROOM! VROOM!*

"Can we go for a ride?" she asked Carlita.

"Sure." Carlita climbed on behind Kate, grabbed the handlebars, and said, "Let's take a quick spin around the heliport."

Carlita quickly released the clutch lever. The front tire lifted off the ground, and the bike did a wheelie as they took off. Kate screamed with excitement as they raced around the heliport, zigzagging between helicopters.

Carlita had Kate twist the throttle, and she pulled a wheelie as well.

"Wow!" Kate screamed with joy.

They pulled over to Harry and Kyle, and Kate got off the bike.

"Thanks, Carlita," Kate said. "That was awesome."

"Jump back into the chopper, kids," Carlita said. They hopped in and sank into the seats.

"What do your parents think of you riding motorcycles and flying helicopters, not to mention being a cyborg?" Kate asked Carlita.

"They're not happy about it, to say the least. They say flying a helicopter is a man's job, and riding motorcycles is too dangerous! And they're right—I died riding my motorcycle. And they wanted me to be an attorney." She stuck a finger in her mouth like she was going to gag. "I went to law school but dropped out and used my tuition money for flight school. I think it was the right decision for me but only you will know if the decision you made today is right for you."

"Wow, Carlita. I like you," Kate said. "Mom and Dad want me to be an attorney too, and they want Kyle to be an engineer. So boring." They all stuck their fingers in their mouths—even Harry—and pretended to gag.

"Yup, you never hear parents say, 'You should be a pilot.' It's always a *standard issue* for boys and girls. And I can tell you're smart. Just listen and do as Harry instructs, and you'll be fine," Carlita said.

"You're a pretty wild girl, Carlita," said Kate.

"Well—an old boyfriend told me something that's always stuck with me: 'Live life on the edge or die on the porch.' Most people live boring lives and then grow old and die on the porch. So take that, for what it's worth."

"Yeah! I'm going to live life on the edge! That reminds me of what my science teacher told me when we were talking about dreams," Kate said. "Life is either a daring adventure or nothing!"

Carlita smiled. "That's the key to life, and you're on a daring adventure. You go, girl."

"Hey, what are these funny-looking pedals on both sides of the floor?" Kyle asked. "Can we pedal the helicopter?" he joked.

"Yeah right!" Machismo replied. "The pedals also help steer the helicopter. By pushing on them, you keep the helicopter flying in a straight line."

"Have you ever pushed the pedals on a piano?" Harry asked the twins.

"Yes, we have one at home. We love playing with it," Kate said.

"By pushing the pedals on the piano, you keep the air pressure continuous and balanced, just like in a helicopter. So think of flying a helicopter like playing a musical instrument. Everything must act in concert, like in the symphonies Mozart and Beethoven wrote."

"Piece of cake, right Kyle?" Kate said.

"Sure sure, sis," Kyle said.

"Come on. Let's roll through the instrument panel real quick," Harry continued, leaning in and pointing to the gauges. "This gauge tells you how fast you're flying: slow, fast, or really, really fast. And this gauge will smile or frown depending on how the chopper feels. The chopper likes to fly when it's cool outside. When it's hot and humid, he struggles to fly."

"Keep it cool," Machismo said. "When it's hot and sticky, I have a hard time breathing."

Carlita took over. "These are your headsets." She handed the twins red headphones that were plugged into the dash, and they put them on. "The headsets allow you to chat with and listen to other pilots as well as the people working at airport control towers."

"Can you hear me, kids?" Machismo asked.

"Yeah," Kate said. "We hear you loud and clear, Machismo."

Machismo said. "We want to know where other choppers and airplanes are when they're flying so we won't collide."

Kate said, "I hear chatter. Chopper tango is requesting permission to land."

"Wait a minute, Kate," Harry said. It's a trap and the crazy Will wants to land. Tell him no, he's not clear to land and to find another heliport."

"Okay, Harry. Sorry, the heliport is not clear today. You must find another place," Kate said.

"Are you sure about that, kid?" Will asked.

"Yes, I am. Now go away!" Kate said sternly.

"What's the problem,with him?" Kyle asked.

"He's that rebelious teenager.—Will, who despises authority and is hell–bent on hurting people like you and me. And until I find a way to eliminate him, I don't want to deal with him," Harry said. "But he will be back."

"Eliminate, really?" Kyle said.

"Yes, he's a very bad kid."

"Okay, these headsets are awesome," Kate said.

"Don't let me forget the most important gauge," Carlita said. "Your *gas* gauge! The chopper is thirsty when it comes to gasoline. Always, always, always make sure the tank is full before takeoff!" She tapped the gas gauge with her index finger.

"Yeah, guys," Machismo said. "There's no reason to autorotate to prevent a crash if you don't have to."

"If the helicopter runs out of gas, are we toast?" Kyle asked Carlita, remembering Harry's crash landing.

"Not quite," she replied. "The helicopter comes equipped with an emergency horn. It makes a loud sound in the cock–pit to alert you that the helicopter needs immediate attention or you could crash and die. It's a cockpit warning noise. It repeats itself until the appropriate action has been taken," Carlita said.

"Wow, how funny," Kate said.

"Even more importantly, you need to keep the engine running just right. If the engine slows down, it might stall and cause you to crash. The horn will remind you when the engine needs throttle. And if you get too low on gas, it will alert you to get ready to autorotate. Although this chopper is an android, it's not perfect. The chopper was designed to land without the motor running, but you must still know the basics!"

"Flying a chopper doesn't sound so easy anymore," Kyle said, looking pale.

Carlita shrugged. "A flight instructor once told me, 'There's nothing to fear but fear itself.' Flying helicopters has its challenges, just like almost anything in life worth doing. Just remember to stay cool, calm, and collected in the face of danger. And besides, you can easily learn autorotation like everyone else. When the engine stops, the rotor will spin through the air—you hope—allowing the chopper to come in for a landing."

"Really? Boy, I feel better now," Kyle said.

"Machismo pitched in. "I have an idea. Let's practice autorotation."

"Okay, sounds like fun," Kate said with a grin. Kyle punched the air. "Way cool! We're going flying!"

"First take a look at the wind pants flying on the pole over the heliport roof," Machismo said.

"You'll want to take off with the wind in your face. Now turn the key."

"Watch your gauges as we warm up, and plant your feet firmly on the pedals," Machismo instructed. "Right hand on the cyclic, left hand on the collective. Kate, gently pull up on the collective and get this chopper off the ground."

"Oh," Kate said. "We're lifting off. Wow, what a weird feeling!"

"Now gently push each of the pedals with the same pressure and keep us straight."

Kate stretched her legs as far as she could in order to push the pedals and not slide off the seat.

"Does it feel like your stomach is in your mouth?" Machismo asked. "That feeling will pass."

"Yes, I have that exact feeling," Kate said, looking queasy.

Kate and Kyle were airborne at one-thousand feet above the heliport when Machismo made an announcement. "I'm going to pretend to run out of gas, turn off the engine, and let you do an autorotation. Hold onto the stick, Kate, and gently lower the collective and roll off the throttle. That'll result in a safe landing. Watch your gauges, and keep the nose up. More right pedal! We're coming in too fast! We're going to crash!"

"Can you give me a little help here, Machismo?" Kate shouted, as the ground approached ever too quickly. Kyle flashed her a terrified look.

"Come on. Man up, kid," Billy Bob teased. He was sitting on Kate's right shoulder. "Be strong. Be brave like me. You can do it."

"Hey, where did you come from? Anyway, I'm just a kid. Give me a break!" Suddenly, Kate grabbed a barf bag and threw up.

"Jeez, kid. You gonna be alright?" Machismo asked.

"Yeah, I'm fine," Kate said, wiping her mouth.

"Get lost, Billy Bob," Machismo said. "When was a bumblebee ever strong or brave?"

As everyone laughed, Machismo told Kate, "I turned the engine back on because we had some room for error.

I have the controls now, so you can let go of the cyclic stick. Good thing we were just practicing, or this could have gotten really ugly." He flew back up to one thousand feet above the heliport to demonstrate the autorotation again. Kate sat frozen and pale, with little beads of sweat on her brow. "Okay, Kyle," he continued, "you want to try it this time?"

"Maybe next time," Kyle said.

"Don't be a chicken, Kyle," Kate teased. "Here's a barf bag just for you."

"That's okay," he said, patting her shoulder.

The view from a thousand feet felt like they could see for a thousand miles in each direction on a clear day. The hills were as green as could be and the mountains radiated in the distance.

"Watch as I ease back on the cyclic to bring the nose of the chopper up and ease the collective down," Machismo said. The cyclic stick self-adjusted to its neutral position as they gently glided in and landed. "See how easy that was?"

"It's not that easy, Kyle," Kate said, wiping the sweat off her brow. "Trust me."

Kyle nodded. "I know, sis. I saw you barf, and I can still smell it."

Kate pulled the elastic band on Kyle's underpants and snapped him with it.

"Ow! That stings!" he yelped.

"I have an emergency I gotta take care of, kids. I'll see you down the road, I'm sure," Carlita said, and peeled away, creating a cloud of dust.

Helicopter Huey

Fear no bully!

Harry turned to the twins as they walked away from him. "What are you two talking about?"

"Barfing," Kyle said.

"No more barfing if I'm going to teach you to fly." Harry motioned for them to follow him. "Walk with me down to the other choppers."

As the kids and Harry walked down the warm tarmac, Kyle pointed to a large helicopter. "What's that big green chopper, Harry?"

Harry said, "That's Helicopter Huey."

The large green helicopter was sitting on the warm tarmac away from everyone else. Helicopter Huey fluttered his eyes sleepily and smiled at the twins.

"Don't wake the sleeping giant," Billy Bob joked. "He needs his beauty rest."

"*Yo*, are you talking to me?" Huey asked in a deep, raspy voice as he lit up with a sharp, stern gleam. "I'm Helicopter Huey, king of helicopters, full of stone-cold aluminum!" The large green chopper bellowed and squeaked as he struggled to flex his rotor overhead.

"Wow," Kate said, surprised.

Kyle laughed.

"Yes, that's not all you're full of, you old bucket of bolts," Billy Bob told Huey. "You mean you used to be the king." Billy Bob buzzed around the chopper, flying by everyone's faces and being the pest that he was.

"I'm afraid that's true," Helicopter Huey said with a sigh.

"You sound sad, Helicopter Huey," Kate said.

"That's because I am," Huey said. "I might look like a star-studded chopper, but I'm not the lean, mean fighting machine I once was. I've been replaced by more star-studded choppers, like the young, snooty Astar." Huey sighed. "I'm just a lonely old chopper."

"When were you ever lean, old man?" Billy Bob mumbled.

"Hey, you slack-jawed hillbilly," Huey said, "you might want to watch how much honey you're sucking down before you can't lift your bubble butt off the ground anymore!"

broke into a fit of laughter.

"You know, my geriatric friend, flattery will get you nowhere," Billy Bob said. "It's late. Shouldn't you be off to the old Huey hangar?"

"What's that red liquid on the ground underneath Helicopter Huey?" Kate asked.

"Leakage," Billy Bob said. "Huey, it's way past your hundred-hour under-carriage inspection."

Huey looked embarrassed. Chantal the hummingbird came to his rescue.

"Boys, knock it off!" she said. "You're both a couple of studs in my book. Besides, you've moved on to bigger and better things, Helicopter Huey. And you're a war hero and a decorated veteran. You should be proud."

"Yeah," he said, and began to reminisce. "Those were my glory days. One day my buddies and I came under fire when we were hunting bad guys. We were buzzing above the treetops, and I was sprayed with machine-gun fire." The twins looked shocked. "The bullet entered my crankcase and came out of my manifold. Oh, that was painful—I was hemorrhag-ing oil and sucking air and choking myself to death. My motor seized shortly after that, and I had to autorotate into a minefield. I thought I was a goner. Bullets were flying all over, bombs werebursting, and then everything went silent. Suddenly the sky exploded with fireworks. The Badass Bros showed up, and *wow*, what an entrance they made!" Huey paused for a moment, looking a bit embar–rassed. "Sorry to bore you with my war stories, kids. I get a little carried away once I get going."

"It's fine, Huey," Kyle said, putting his arm around Kate's shoulders. "You're a wounded warrior—and a hero—and we'd love to hear more. But who are the Badass Bros?"

"Those were the days before I became an android. Those bros were my favorite Apache and Cobra helicopters. Windmaker and Striker. Harry will tell you more about them. Anyway, I did earn a Purple Heart when I went down," Helicopter Huey said, gleaming with pride. "However, Chantal is right. I've moved onto bigger and better things. I'm now a semi-retired android who takes secret cargo to undisclosed destinations in the dark of night."

"Hey, I just got a message to pick up Otis. He took a tumble down a hillside and twisted his new bionic leg while he was on a scouting mission for new places to grow our biomass pumpkins," Harry said.

"Can't we help?" Kate pleaded. "We're *empowered* now, and we won't get in the way."

"Okay, we make biomass fuel for our helicopters with the pumpkins. Maybe I should call your folks?" Harry suggested.

"No, please don't," Kate said, "They know we are playing in the park."

"I guess I could use the help," Harry said with a sigh. He glanced at his watch. "Let's take Huey. He's all gassed up and ready to go. He could use a hydraulic line replacement, but it'll have to wait."

Helicopter Huey's face lit up. "Are you sure about this Harry?" Huey asked.

"I'm sure," Harry said.

They all climbed into the helicopter. Kyle jumped into the front as co-pilot, and Kate sat in the back. Harry fired up Huey, and within a few moments, they were flying into the foothills. They approached the American River and saw Otis. He was a beautiful, older black stallion who couldn't stand to be in a corral. He had been recently rebuilt into an android horse who could run at 100 miles per hour when everything was working right.

"I understand his mother-board blew a circuit and he can't walk," Harry said. "We'll lift him out and take him to the big, flat schoolyard not far from here."

"Sounds like a good plan," Kyle said.

Harry radioed ahead to the elementary school to let them know he was bringing Otis to the field. This is a regular school and the children get excited when cyborgs and androids stop by. Harry flew over and circled around and lined up the cable above Otis.

"Looks like they have Otis all suited up in his special sling to be transported," Harry said.

"When will Otis turn into a helicopter like Machismo did?" Kyle asked. He and Kate both laughed.

Harry laughed too. "Soon, we hope. But we 've been working on this experimental android horse for some time and thought we had all the bugs worked out. Apparently that's not the case."

"The river is eating away at the bank Otis is standing on, so there's not a lot of room for error on this side. I'll have to fly underneath those power lines between the bridge and the cliff to pluck him out. This is going to be tricky!"

The technicians activated Otis's communication module so he could communicate with Harry.

"How's it going, Otis?" Harry said.

"You know me, Harry. I've gotten myself into a jam again with this new android technology. Thanks for coming, and could you hurry? I understand you have children with you, though. I thought you learned your lesson last time."

"Okay, are you ready to take flight?

"Yes, Harry, but I think I might have found a new fuel reserve," Otis said.

"Great. Let's talk about that later."

The cable was clipped to Otis's harness, and Harry pulled up on the collective. As the chopper rose, the slack was taken up, and the horse harness tightened.

"I hope you know what you're doing up there. Your rotor wash is creating a sandstorm." As the horse harness squeezed Otis's ribcage, he grunted, farted and felt like he was getting a wedgie.

"Hey, what's with the buzzing around my head? Is there a bee near me? You know I hate bees." Otis snorted again and shook his head. "He landed on my head! He's crawling around my ears and now my eyes. He's getting ready to sting me! I'm in a tight spot here, and I'm going to kick somebody. Get your fat butt-cheeks off my face, bee!" While Otis was yelling, The kids couldn't stop laughing.

"Calm down," Harry said. "It's just Billy Bob horsing around. Bugger off, Billy Bob!"

"Oh, my god, what stinks?" Otis exclaimed. "Did Billy Bob poop on my face?"

"No, I just passed a lot of gas," Billy Bob said, laughing hysterically.

"Oh, man, bee farts are the worst. Get the heck out of here!" Otis demanded. "You're making my eyes sting!"

"Okay, already. We all need a little horse humor now and then," Billy Bob said, still laughing. "Sorry, Otis. I didn't mean to scare you. Just trying to ease the tension."

"Alright, then, giddy-up," Otis said, as he was lifted off the ground.

"Darn it, I didn't think those power lines in front of us would be a problem. I did not anticipate flying through them or above them," Harry said.

"How are you going to get through them?" Kate asked. "Can you actually fly underneath them?"

"No problem," Harry said.

Kyle frowned. "I don't know. I'm scared."

Helicopter Huey, who'd been fairly quiet all this time, became concerned as they approached the power lines with Otis on a hundred-foot cable. "We need to act fast," he said, "or we might tangle the rotor in the power lines and crash. We might even slam Otis into the rocks!"

"W-watch it, Harry!" Kate stuttered. "I think you're getting too close for comfort. Maybe you should back off your plan?"

"If you don't, we might become toast!" Kyle said.

As Harry tried to guide the chopper between the bridge and the power lines, he realized he couldn't move forward or backward without snagging the lines or smacking the bridge. "If push comes to shove, one flick of this switch and Otis will fall into the river. I prefer plan B," he said. "I'm going to cut the lines with my hand rotors. This will be tight because I'll have to stand on the strut. The strut supports the helicopter when it's on the ground, like your foot does when you stand up. I'll secure my footing and then cut the power line. Kyle, you'll need to rotate the chopper to the right, with a lot of right pedal. Are you ready?"

"Sure, Harry. No problem," Kyle replied, "as long as I don't have to autorotate!"

"Let me do this, now that I'm experienced at autorotation," Kate said.

Harry looked at Kate and then at Kyle. "Maybe your sister's right, Kyle."

"No, I got this, and I won't barf like Kate did."

"Okay, but don't screw this up, kid. Our lives are at stake," Harry said. "Take the cyclic stick, hold the collective and plant your feet firmly on the pedals. Remember, you're empowered!"

"Okay. Got it, Harry."

Harry opened the door, climbed out, and stood on the skid. "Kyle," he said, "push the right pedal to the floor and turn the body of the chopper toward the power lines." He signaled Kyle, who swung the helicopter around, bringing it in close to the power lines. Harry stretched his left-hand rotor out and held onto the door of the helicopter with his right hand. He made his slice. The power lines dropped and slapped the skid, sending static electricity throughout the chopper and making everyone's hair stand on end.

Then the chopper jerked back and forth, scaring Kyle.

"Kate," Kyle said, "What just happened?"

"It's Will, he's trying to get into the chopper and kill you both," Harry said. "He's the bad kid that blackened your eyes in the park. Kate, climb into the front seat and help your brother fly."

Kate climbed into the front seat and encouraged Kyle to keep the chopper steady. Harry was on one side of the helicopter, and Will was on the other side. He started bang–ing on the door. "That's what you get for not letting me land!" Will said. Both Kate and Kyle looked down through the window and saw the river one hundred feet below. "We're not going swimming today," Kate said."

"Open the door and let me in!" Will yelled.

"Ignore him, Kyle, you can do this," Kate said, wiping a bead of sweat off his brow.

"Yeah, it's Will from the park. He has on his AS shirt and his purple hat turned backward. I owe him a black eye!" Kyle said.

"Is everything alright up there?" Otis asked, "It seems we have encountered some turbulence."

"Yes, we have an uninvited guest. Will wants in," Kate said.

"Do not let him in," Harry said. "He will crash the helicopter."

Just then, Kyle's foot slipped off the other pedal, and the chopper shifted to the left. Harry lost his grip on the door, making his feet slide off the skid. He was barely able to grab the skid with his arm. He just avoided getting sucked into the tail rotor which was spinning at two hundred miles per hour. He swung under the chopper, grabbed the cold steel cable, and slid down onto Otis.

THUMP! "Surprise, it's me!" Harry said.

"I know, but we have unwelcome company."

"I know and I'll be right back," Harry said.

Harry engaged his hand rotors, flew over Otis to the top of the chopper, grabbed Will by his feet and pulled him off the chopper. They were both tumbling through the air when Harry shot Will with a laser bolt and stunned him. He fell into the river and floated down a way. Harry flew back to the chopper and landed back on Otis. "Problem solved for now," Harry said.

"That was close, Harry. He almost got to the kids," Otis said."

Harry clicked the microphone on his headset. "Kyle, I'm down here with Otis. Can you two kids take us to the schoolyard?"

"No problem, Harry," Kyle said. "We'll take care of it."

As they approached the schoolyard, Huey's leaking hydraulic line blew out, and steering the helicopter became next to impossible. Down below, the school children cheered, "Otis! Otis! Otis!"

Kyle clicked into Harry's headset. "Harry, we have a problem. I think the hydraulic line has blown out. I can barely steer the chopper."

"Yes, I see red liquid spraying out all over the place," Harry said. "You'll need to release the cable that Otis is attached to. When we're fifty feet off the ground, lower the collective and release the cable when I tell you to."

"Got it, Harry," Kyle said.

"Roger that," Kate replied.

"Otis," Harry said, "we have a slight problem with the hydraulics. Kyle is going to release you momentarily, so be ready to land."

"Ten-four, Harry. I'll do the best I can, although I can't move real well," Otis said.

"You'll feel the ground beneath you shortly. Look smart for your brief moment of fame, Otis. Okay, Kyle, release the cable with the orange button, and then set Huey down nice and easy. I'll repair the hydraulic line."

"Okay, Harry," Kyle said.

Otis pointed his head forward, flared his tail and stood like a statue

Kyle and Kate maneuvered the chopper to the grass in the schoolyard, guiding Otis to a smooth landing. After they released the cable, Harry climbed off Otis and unhooked him. Kyle gracefully landed the chopper not far from them. All the school kids gathered around Otis, petting him and lavishing him with affection. However, the children didn't know he was an android since he seemed perfectly real.

Harry climbed inside the cockpit and slapped Kyle on the back. "Nice job for a ten-year-old. Thanks for staying cool, calm, and collected. You too, Kate." He grabbed a replacement hydraulic line from the back seat and repaired the malfunction within a few minutes.

"Thanks for the lift," Otis graciously told Harry.

"No problem, mate. The technicians should have you good as new before you know it. You will be running your tail off until we need you again."

"Sure thing, dude!" Otis said and flared his black tail.

Harry climbed back inside the cockpit and took the pilot seat then flew them all back to the heliport, where they landed safely. He checked his watch. "This was just supposed to be a demonstration about how Huey still has talent even though he's an old fart. But thanks for your help, you two."

"Yeah, that was Will that attacked us in the park!" Kate said.

"I figured that. He's been our number one trouble-maker for some time," Harry said.

"Yeah, that was pretty scary with Will trying to get in the chopper. We thought we might die," Kyle said.

"I know, and I'm sorry. It's okay if you want to go home now. Coin flip or not."

"Nope, we are committed to this adventure. Right, Kyle?"

"Sure, Kate. That was dangerous but exihilarating!"

As they exited the chopper, Kyle was surprised by a large piece of steel shaped like giant jaws with big teeth. As he walked by, the jaws opened and snapped shut very fast.

Kyle jumped. "What the heck is that thing?"

"That's Jaws," Harry explained. "When he is attached to the chopper on a cable, he digs dirt from the side of the Sierra Mountains with his powerful jaws. Now he sets power poles, but in days past, he helped dredge rivers for gold."

"Hey, Jaws," Kyle said, grinning. "I see dredging rivers has been good to you, based on your gold tooth."

"Aye, lad. You might say that," Jaws said, his gold tooth sparkling in the sun. "And you know what else, my little friend? I can swallow children who spy and trespass on private property."

The twins looked at each other—terrified. Jaws let out a booming laugh. *Gotcha!* Just kidding. "I wouldn't swallow a kid. I'd rather pick up cars off the freeway when there is an accident."

The kids slowly walked backward. "Um…okay. Can we…uh…check out some other helicopters?" Kyle asked, looking nervously back at Jaws.

"Don't worry about Jaws," Harry said. "He's just messing with you."

Kate pointed and said, "Um…can we look at that black and white helicopter over there?"

"Sure thing," Harry said. He led them over to the chopper and opened the white door. This is Turbo."

The twins climbed in, slammed the door behind them, locked it and took their seats. Harry sat in the pilot seat. Kate took the co-pilot seat, and Kyle was in the back. Kyle pointed out the square window. "Phew. That was close," he said, wiping his forehead. "I don't trust that Jaws. I think he wants to eat us."

Speeding through Time

Villains hate, heroes congratulate.

Kate looked through the window and saw Chantal the hummingbird flying upside down.

"So what do you think?" Chantal sang. "Pretty cool, eh? As you know, hummingbirds can fly upside down."

"There goes Little Miss Perfect," Billy Bob shouted. "Show-off!"

"You know, slack jaw, you're just jealous because I have a fine-tuned body that can fly circles around your jelly belly." Chantal put her wing tips on her hips and pointed her long, narrow beak in the air.

"Maybe you could show us some helicopters that can fly upside down," Kate said.

"Well…that's a little complicated," Harry said.

Kate raised an eyebrow. "What do you mean?"

"It can be done, and it's incredibly fun. But it requires circumventing the natural laws of physics."

"Well, that does sound hard and dangerous, but let's do it anyway!" Kate exclaimed.

"Let me tell you a little story," Harry said. "One day I was experimenting with a new helicopter that I had built. It's just about the fastest helicopter ever. When I started accelerating in a continuous loop at high speed, everything suddenly got really dark! My inertia had created a gravity vortex, and I had entered a black hole."

The twins listened in disbelief as Harry went on, speaking in a serious tone. "And the weirdest thing happened when I entered the black hole. The rotor blade immediately stopped and began to spin backward at the rate of speed of 186,000 miles per second, which is the speed of light and the speed of time travel. I was in a time warp— the bending of time—and I actually went back in time."

"How far back?" Kate blurted out, her eyes wide.

"To the birth of the helicopter: five-hundred years ago! I landed in Florence, Italy, near an old stone structure. It turned out to be his design studio for inventions. Even back then the city was quite large with many grey stone structures."

"Whose design studio?" Kate asked.

"Leonardo da Vinci's!"

"No way!" Kyle said.

"Yes way," Harry said. "I knocked on the door. This old gent opened it and glared at me, but he didn't appear to be surprised to see me."

Kate asked, "What did he look like?"

"Leonardo had a wizardly look to him. He was dressed in a black robe, and his matted hair matched the scraggly beard that surrounded his face. I watched as he designed his time-machine prototype. His helicopter design wasn't for a helicopter after all, as everyone thinks. It was a vehicle to time-travel with, but it lacked a power source."

"That makes sense. His design looks nothing like a helicopter," Kate said.

"And who better to create a time machine than Leonardo da Vinci?" Harry continued.

"Talk about a real genius! What didn't that Renaissance man know how to do? Leo had a bloody short attention span, though. He'd bounce from working on his time machine to his hang glider, then to his parachute, then back to his time machine, and then to his paintings. However, he spent twenty-five years pursuing his elusive dream of flight and couldn't make it work."

"That's amazing," Kate said. "I can't believe it."

"Yes, he shared so much with me," Harry said, smiling. "He showed me the diagrams for his flying machine, but there was something odd about them. I only wish I'd had more time to study them. When I showed him my helicopter, it blew his mind. He said it was exactly what he was working on, but he knew he didn't have five-hundred years to figure it out. He thanked me for bringing his dream to fruition."

"Sitting next to his diagrams was a metallic cylinder," Harry went on. "I went to pick it up, but Leonardo grabbed my hand and said no. I asked what it was for, and he said it was his dream bank, where all his dreams-past and present—started. He wrote down all his dreams on slips of parchment paper, put them into his dream bank and worked tirelessly to make them come true. The words *"Dream It, Learn It, Do It,"* were engraved on the outside. However, Leonardo surprised me as I left. He tapped me on the shoulder, handed me his dream bank, and said, "My dreams are complete. You can use this for your own dreams. And one day, when you meet someone who needs it more than you do, you must pass it on. Make sure it doesn't end up in the hands of a non-believer, since a person like that can destroy your dreams. You have to believe in yourself, Harry, because nobody else will! This dream bank is the key to your future. Don't lose it."

The children now appeared to be in a trance.

"Unbelievable!" Kate said. "Where is the dream bank now?"

"In a safe place," Harry said. "My dreams came to life through the dream bank. I just wrote my dreams down and put them in da Vinci's dream bank. After many years of focus and hard work, they took on a life of their own. The dream bank picks up vibrations from the dream itself and will only nurture good dreams—it can't be used to do bad things. I only wish I'd had one when I was your age so I could have gotten a head start on my dreams."

"Can you tell us more about the time machine?" Kyle asked.

"That's it!" Kate whispered in Kyle's ear. "The time-machine helicopter must be the helicopter our science teacher told us about. That has to be it! *The one that can fly like no other.*"

"Anyway, sounds like Jackaroo is approaching. It's that time of the day, and he needs gas. He's a big part of the team. Not just an eye in the sky but a tough guy. We'll talk about this again, but keep it to yourselves, would you? I can't tell you how much trouble the world would be in if the wrong people found out about it. Like Will!"

"Okay Harry, we won't tell anyone," Kate said. She poked Kyle and whispered, "Like kids can keep a secret!" And they exited the chopper.

Jackaroo

Don't judge—No one is perfect!

The twins looked up and listened but didn't see or hear a chopper approaching. They watched for Jackaroo in the far distance.

"Jackaroo," Harry said into his radio. Harry turned his back and whispered. "You're clear to land, but I have these children with me. Maybe Borg could give them the once-over to make sure they aren't spies for Will."

"Sure, Harry. If they are spies, Borg will sniff them out."

The sound of the chopper continued to grow louder and louder as it approached.

"Jackaroo, what kind of name is that?" Kate laughed.

"Hey!" Kyle yelled. "Looks like smoke is coming out of the helicopter."

Kate slapped Harry on the shoulder and nudged Kyle. The red, blue and white chopper approached to land. "This looks all too familiar," she said, laughing.

"Real funny, kid. Keep it up, and Jaws will be giving the lesson."

Borg, the co-pilot dog, radioed for help. He barked into the headset microphone: three quick barks for 911, followed by more barks. "Mayday! Mayday!" The cockpit is full of smoke and I can't read the instrument panel. I need to land the chopper now! Bark me in, would you?" Borg yelped.

Harry barked his commands to Borg. "Bark, bark, bark...blimey, remember your ABCs!"

Borg could barely see due to all the smoke and started hacking.

"Kyle laughed. "His dog is going to land the chopper?"

"Come on, Harry. Get real!" Kate laughed. "Is he really a dog or one of your smart machines?"

"Yup, kid," Harry said. "He's a cyborg dog and he is trained for just such an event."

"Wow," Kate said, poking Kyle in the arm. "This gives new meaning to the phrase 'rescue dog.' "

"Are you okay?" Harry asked Borg.

"Ten-four, Harry. I'm just a little choked up at the moment."

Harry tried to reassure him. "Easy, bring her in for a nice, smooth landing. Straighten out the chopper. More left pedal. Easy," he continued. "You almost have it. No, you don't have it. *Abort!* No! You almost hit Helicopter Huey!"

Borg pulled up, cleared Helicopter Huey, and began to pant. "Sorry, I can't see clearly right now." He circled around and made another attempt to land.

"Your approach looks great," Harry said. "Now land the chopper before you crash it!"

Borg had one paw on the stick and one on the collective. Harry guided him in for an almost perfect landing. Borg landed the chopper, skidding twenty feet to a stop.

"Jackaroo taught you well," Harry said.

"No worries, mate!" Borg barked.

Borg exited the chopper and greeted Harry and the twins. Borg was jumping up and down and happy to see everyone. He panted with excitement, his sloppy tongue swinging around. Borg looked just like a German shepherd. He was the same size and had black and tan fur, but he had more black around his nose and mouth.

"G'day, Harry," Jackaroo said.

"Bingo bongo, Jackaroo. Good thing you had Borg with you today. What happened up there?"

"We hit some wind turbulence. Silly me, I didn't buckle up, and I was bounced around and got knocked out."

Jackaroo was a tall Aussie. He was sporting a new tan, and looked like he hadn't shaved in a couple of days. He was wearing just white underpants, a gold chain, aviator glasses, cowboy boots and a cowboy hat. He signaled for Borg, who waltzed over to the kids and began to sniff them.

"How come you don't wear pants Jackaroo?" Kyle asked, snickering.

"This Aussie just doesn't like pants. As you might know, it gets really hot Down Under. I'm a better pilot when I feel the wind blowing, which makes me more aerodynamic," Jackaroo said.

"Don't worry about Jackaroo, kids. He's a little odd." Harry said. "However he is as tough as it comes. He's as strong as an ox, as you can tell by his muscles."

The children and Harry laughed.

"Hey, what's up with the dog?" Kate asked. "Why is he sniffing us so much?"

"Get your nose out of my butt, dog," Kyle said, Borg lifted his leg and tinkled on Kyle's pant leg. Kate laughed hysterically until Borg peed on *her* leg. Kyle and Harry laughed and fist-bumped each other.

"What the…?" Kate said, kicking Borg away.

Borg snarled, bared his teeth, and grabbed Kate's pant leg. A tug-of-war ensued as Harry and Kyle laughed even harder.

"Jackaroo!" Kate shouted. "Get your dog off me!"

"Somebody is having a bad day! Borg, give the kid a break. She's gonna pee her pants if you don't stop." He turned to Kate. "That's just his sign of approval." Jackaroo looked at Harry and gave the okay sign to tell him that the kids weren't spies. Usually spies had a nervous scent that told Borg if they couldn't be trusted and had to be eliminated."

"Okay, kids, you have now been formally introduced to Mr. Flying Underpants," Harry said. "Jackaroo, this is Kate and Kyle."

"Nice to meet you, Jackaroo," Kate said, as he squeezed her hand. "Nice boots," she added, giggling at his underpants.

Kyle extended his hand and shook Jackaroo's hand as well. "Can we see the inside of your chopper?" he asked.

"Sure. Jump in and take a peek. He's a real beaut," Jackaroo said, motioning for the twins to climb in.

"Nice chopper, Jackaroo," Kyle said. "It smells a little smoky, but more like a dog. I think your chopper needs a bath." The twins laughed and snuggled down into the large pilot seats.

"That's my Borg," Jackaroo said, patting the dog on the head. As he stood next to the chopper, he leaned in to talk to the kids.

"What are you guys talking about?" Harry asked.

"Just going over the controls," Jackaroo said.

"What exactly do you do, Jackaroo?" asked Kyle. "And are you a cyborg too?"

"Oh, yeah. A cyborg with an eye in the sky, which makes me a vital asset to the team. Besides, I'm always looking for a news story, and I'm also on the lookout for bullies and the leader of the Kommando Kids, " Jackaroo said.

"We met Will. He tried to crash Huey with us at the controls!"

"Wow! There's the news story I've been looking for all day to write up in our daily blog. The team needs to know what kind of trouble he is up to. I'm glad you are okay."

"What kind of dog is Borg, and how did he get that name?" I guess he's sorta like a superhero dog since he saved your life," Kyle said.

"You're right! He's a German Shepard, and he is my co-pilot. He was killed by a bad dude and was rebuilt into a cyborg, which is how he got his name," Jackaroo said.

"Where did you get him?" Kyle asked.

"Harry gave him to me from one of his tours of duty," Jackaroo said, smiling with pride. "Borg took a bullet when Harry was in a firefight. He saved Harry's life. Now he's semi-retired." Jackaroo smiled. "Borg is trained to sniff out stink bombs, spies and bullies. I take care of my Borg and he takes care of me."

"Did Borg earn a Purple Heart?" Kyle asked.

"Yes," Harry said. "A troublemaker managed to jump me from behind. I flipped him onto his back, and even though he'd taken a bullet to the ribcage, Borg leapt into action and jumped on the guy. He kept him pinned down. and growled into the guy's face, waiting for my command. The guy was crying like a little schoolgirl. I tied him up and took him prisoner earning Borg his Purple Heart. But, Borg died shortly afterward."

"Holy cow," Kyle said. "What a story. "Can Borg fly like us?"

"Sure he can. Hey Borg, fly for the twins."

Borg's tail started to spin like a rotor and he was off in seconds with his front legs stretched out with hand rotors.

"Oh my god, how cool is that!" Kate said. "You and Borg sure have been through a lot, Harry."

"Anyway, I thought Jackaroo could use Borg's help for a while." Harry winked at Jackaroo.

"Sorry…I didn't know Borg was a hero," Kate said. "Come here, Borg." As Borg ran over, Kate knelt down to greet him. Borg knocked her down in a friendly manner and licked her face.

"Watch your neck, Kate," Jackaroo said with a laugh, walking over to Harry.

"What kind of chopper is this, Jackaroo?" Kyle asked, pointing to the chopper. "It looks more sleek and stylish than most helicopters."

"This is Astar, and his ego is larger than life," Jackaroo said. "He thinks he's a celebrity."

"You know it! I'm a star in the sky!" Astar said. "I'm proud to be a Euro Chopper rather than a Yankee. I was made to outshine all the other choppers."

The twins chuckled.

"That's the chopper Huey talked about, eh, Harry?" Kyle said.

"Yup, that's him alright," Harry said.

"*Huey*, that washed-up rust-bucket of bolts? Did he trash-talk me?" Astar said.

Jackaroo shrugged. "I'm sure he did. Sorry, kids—Astar's a little sensitive and preoccupied with himself. You know how Brits can be. I'm sure you two would like to learn more about Astar," he continued, "but he and I really must be moving on. We'll come back and chat another time." He turned to Astar. "Are you ready, Astar?"

"Not quite," Astar said. "Why don't you put some pants on?" You're an embarrassment to the great country I stand for."

"Who does he think he is?" Kate said, rolling her eyes.

"You're all gassed up, Jackaroo. Now get airborne before Astar makes tonight's news blog," Harry said with a chuckle, slapping Jackaroo on the shoulder.

Mr. Flying Underpants and Borg jumped into the chopper and were airborne in minutes just as Carlita and Rauquita, the Life Flight chopper, circled around a couple of times before setting down on the tarmac.

Carlita and Rauquita

Buddies not bullies!

Carlita exited the chopper. As she took off her flight helmet, her long, shiny black hair fell down to the middle of her back. She sauntered over to Harry and the twins, running her hand through her hair like a starlet.

"Hello, love," she said, greeting Harry with a kiss on the cheek. "How is my prince charming?"

"Wonderful, princess," Harry said, in turn, kissing her on the cheek.

"Oh, my god," Kyle said, blushing. "I love your black outfit."

"It's the same outfit she was wearing before, Kyle! Stop flirting," Kate said. "Leave that to Harry. Carlita, can you tell us something about your chopper?"

"Sure. She's called Rauquita but is a Life Flight chopper and she's my baby. And the great thing about her is that she's an emergency room in the sky," Carlita said. "When bullies strike, Life Flight can fly into situations that are hard to get to." She turned to Harry. "We had a call that Jackaroo made a crash landing. Is everything okay?"

"All is well. Nothing serious, thanks to Borg," Harry said.

"Good thing," Carlita said.

"That dog bit me!" complained Kate.

Carlita laughed. "So I heard, but no harm done."

Kyle pointed at Carlita's helicopter. "Is that chopper fast?"

"Darn toot-in, kid," said Rauquita interrupting the conversation. "All of us androids have jet engines that make us really fast. Although I'm getting off-track, if a cyborg loses a limb or something worse, we can repair them and get them on their way."

"Would you like to see inside?" Carlita asked them.

"Sure," Kate said.

"Oh no, sorry.—My bad. I gotta run. I just heard some chatter over the radio about Will and his gang causing havoc. They created a car pileup on Highway 101."

"What happened?" Kate said.

"These punks think it's funny to shut down the freeway and terrorize the adults. But it's more about getting Harry's attention. So we extend our services to clean up the mess. And maybe do battle with Will and his gang of Kommandos."

Kate whispered, "Rauquita, do you know anything about Harry's time machine?"

"Yes, she's a sight to behold, and one of the finest androids ever!" Rauquita said. "You'd really enjoy flying her."

Hearing them talk about the time machine, Carlita leaned in and told Rauquita, "Like I said, it's time to go."

Rauquita sighed. "I have to be moving on now," she told Kate and Kyle. "Work, work, work."

"Can we come with you?" asked Kyle.

"That's up to Harry—he's the boss, you know," Carlita said.

Harry hesitated, looked at his watch and then glanced at the twins. "Why not?" he said. "Jump in and buckle up."

"Ten-four," The twins replied. The kids were amazed with what they saw. It looked like a scientific laboratory inside, with weird life support machines.

Harry and Carlita climbed inside and snickered at each other. Carlita fired up Rauquita, and they were in the sky in no time. As Carlita approached the pileup on the freeway, Harry spotted Helicopter Huey and Jaws removing cars from the scene of the accident. Jackaroo and Borg raced over for the breaking story and landed before the authorities got there, directing the choppers as they approached. The Komando Kid had laid the trap and was waiting for the right time to strike.

"Hey, Helicopter Huey," Harry said through his head-set, "can you guys clear some cars to make a landing pad.

"Will do," Huey said. "We have a handful of cars left to clear, but Jaws is beginning to lose his grip on the roof of that mangled white car."

"Look at him salivating," Kyle said. "He's really trying to hold on." Large drops of saliva were dropping to the ground.

Just then, Will struck! He flew into Jaws, forcing the car to swing in the path of Jackaroo and Borg. The car slid out of Jaws's mouth and fell toward Jackaroo and Borg.

"Watch out below, everyone. Incoming!" Harry yelled through his loudspeaker. "Will has struck."

"I got this," Jackaroo said. He looked up as he saw the car coming towards him and Borg but caught it in his arms. He then threw the car at Will and his gang, hitting them all like bowling pins.

"Sorry, guys. We can thank our favorite juvenile delinquent for this chaos," Huey said. "Thank you, Jackaroo!" Huey said on the loudspeaker.

"No worries, mate," Jackaroo yelled back. "If we were Down Under, we would feed these punks to the crocs."

"That was close, Jaws," Harry said, "but we have some room to land now. I count ten cars still piled up down there. It's quite a mess." He shook his head. "I understand Will cut off a sixteen-year-old girl who just got her license and slammed straight into a portapotty sitting near the side of the road. This caused her car to slide sideways and into another car, creating a huge traffic jam." The twins looked over at the collision and saw several people sitting on the side of the road.

"You're not going to barf again, are you, Kate?"

"No, but if I do, I'll aim for your back!"

"Very funny," Kyle said and made a gagging sound.

As Carlita was guiding the chopper down to the highway, Will came crashing into Rauquita's side which caused them to crash onto several empty cars. The chopper made a loud crunching sound of metal breaking when it hit the cars.

"Is everyone okay?" Carlita asked. "Maybe Jaws can grab him!"

"Yes," Kate and Kyle said. "Just a little shook up," explained Kate.

"I'm fine," Harry said.

"Do you see Will, Harry? It's a trap as Will is looking for Kate and Kyle, and I'm sure he and his gang aren't far away," Carlita said.

"There they are," Jackaroo radioed. "Above you at twelve o'clock! Three boys and three girls, and they have white t-shirts with the letters AS tucked into their blue Levis. The boys have boots and the girls have purple tennis shoes like their leader. And they all have purple baseball caps turned backward."

Harry and Carlita jumped into action and started firing their laser bolts at Will and his gang. They were stunned but kept coming. As Harry and Carlita were focused on Will, two of his gang landed next to Rauquita and climbed into the damaged chopper.

"Carlita, bait Will and guide him to Jaws so he can chomp on him," Harry said.

Jaws' mouth was wide open as Carlita guided Will near Harry and flew into him, pushing him into his mouth. Jaws closed his mouth with half of Will inside. Will screamed for his friends to help him. The three girls came and tried to force open Jaws' mouth as Carlita and Harry fought them off. But one girl was quite strong and was able to open Jaws' mouth just enough so Will could escape.

"Come with us!" a 13-year-old boy demanded, looking at Kate.

"No way!" Kate said.

"Let's get him!" Kate and Kyle both jumped on the 13-year-old but he kicked them off quickly. Then Borg jumped onto the back of one of the punks and sank his sharp teeth into the back of his head. This exposed wires and circuits, which caused sparks to fly and made the punk immobile for a moment.

Carlita landed and lasered both teenagers. They were both stunned and stumbled out of the chopper. One teenager grabbed the injured teenager and flew off toward Will who was waiting beyond the wrecked cars. Will took the arm of the injured kid and put it around his neck but couldn't get airborne.

That's when Jackaroo ran over and grabbed Will. He tried to wrestle him to the ground. "Hold still, you little brat!" But Will's strength was no match for Jackaroo and he broke free. Will rolled out from Jackaroo's grip and punched him in the face. Will began to walk away and turned towards Jackaroo.

"You know, boy," said Jackaroo. "Down Under, it isn't the crocs you have to worry about, it's the Black Jungle Swamp. It's full of quicksand and crocs! Let this be a warning: if you keep this charade of yours up with picking on people, I'm going take you Down Under and stick you in the middle of that swamp!"

"Just try it, old man!" called Will. And he flew off.

"Wow, that was close, Jackaroo," Kate yelped.

Carlita flew in and landed and did Harry. "I'm sorry I didn't get to you sooner," Carlita said.

"Everyone okay?" Harry asked as he poked his head through the door.

"We are fine." Kate said,

"I think we are getting the hang of this superhero training. We aren't as scared as we were at first," Kyle said.

"How are you?" Carlita said to Rauquita, who had smoke trailing out of the engine.

"Well, I'll manage. I'm a little banged up. Being an android has its pluses, though. I can have a few blown circuit boards replaced and be back in the air in no time. I'll have Jaws give me a lift back to base, if that's okay with you Harry."

"Oh, sure. That's the spirit," Harry said.

"I'll call my cybertruck and have it pick us up in no time." He opened an app on his phone and pushed a button. Within a few minutes his cybertruck landed with rocket thrusters, just like a rocket ship, and lowered to the ground, and the doors opened.

"Cool truck, Harry," Kyle said. "No door handles?"

"Nope, it knows it's me, and all is good."

"Climb in, everybody, and let's have some fun!" Harry burned rubber and squealed his tires as they peeled off with smoke floating through the air.

"Wow, this is as fast as the chopper!" Kyle said.

Kate's ears perked up as she heard something in the distance. "Sirens!" she shouted.

Sam tHE Man

This is a no-bully zone!

Back at base Harry went to take a call from dispatch. After a minute, he returned and said, "Listen, I need to apprehend a bad guy who stole a new torch–red electric Roadster. As superheroes, you need to be prepared at a moment's notice to put your life in harm's way."

"You can count on us, Harry. Cool!" Kate said. "Let's get the bad guy."

Harry pointed to a large yellow and black helicopter. on the tarmac."This is Sam the Man, climb in, kids," Harry said. The twins ran up and grabbed the door handles.

Kyle said to Kate, "Wow, this is one bad-looking chopper."

"Not so fast, kids," Sam the Man said. "How do I know, you have authorization?"

"It's okay," Harry said. "They're the Copter Kids in training."

"What are you?" Kate asked. "Some kind of copter cop?"

Sam had graduated at the top of his class from the android police academy and had a huge ego.

"We'll talk about it later," Sam said in a stern voice. "We need to go catch us a troublemaker. Climb in, sit down, and buckle up. I'll do the talking." After a moment, he added, "Kids, I might look big and bad, but that's only to remind people I can bring the pain if I have to. Stay in line, and you'll be okay with me."

"Don't scare them, Sam," Harry said.

"What's Sam talking about, Harry?" Kyle asked, as he strapped himself into the co-pilot seat. Harry and Sam ignored him. Kate sat in the back as Harry started up Sam and did a quick pre-flight check. As they lifted off, The twins noticed the many different controls and radios.

"Does anyone see the red Roadster?" Harry asked once they were over the freeway.

"Yeah, I see it," Kyle said. "It's ahead of us in the fast lane!"

Kate leaned forward to get a better look. "Wow! Did you see that?" she said. "The Roadster cut off a school bus. It flipped over and it's sliding down the freeway."

Harry radioed Carlita. "We have an emergency in progress on the freeway near the rest stop exit that needs your immediate attention. A school bus has crashed."

"Ten-four, Harry. Be there in a flash," Carlita said.

"Get him, Harry," Kyle said. "He's weaving in and out of traffic."

"What the…? *That's Carlita's new electric Roadster!* It's such a cool car, with massive horsepower and rocket thrusters that can take the car from zero to sixty in one second! Oh, man, I bet he's going to wreck it," Harry shouted.

"How do you know it's hers'?" Kate asked.

"Her license plate. It's C A R L I T A"

"Wow, that *is* such a beautiful car! I wish I had one," Kate said. "And it matches her motorcycle."

"He must have stolen it from the shop while it was being serviced. I don't think he knows we have him in sight," Harry said. "We need to get this guy behind bars before he hurts anyone else."

They were following the driver from about two hundred feet in the air.

"Maybe I should open up on him with my new laser-gun," Sam said.

"No, too much firepower. That will destroy her car," Harry said.

"I'll show you something about this bad-boy Roadster most people don't know. I can control it by with my smartphone like my cybertuck. First, I'll lock the doors, BAM! Second, I'll deploy the airbags and stop the car," Harry said. Harry deployed the airbags and stopped the car. It screeched to a halt. The passengers jerked forward into the airbags. "Now I'll open the doors with a touch on my smartphone." The doors opened and a guy and a girl stumbled out.

Harry and the team swooped down and landed. Harry exited the chopper. The driver attempted to run from the car, but tripped and fell on his face. "You're busted, dude!" Sam shouted. "Lie face-down on the ground, and let me see your hands! Let me see your hands!" The driver and the girl both lay down. The guy rolled over with a big smile on his face and sprung to his feet.

"It's Will!" Harry said. "And he has his crazy girl-friend with him. It's a trap, kids. Stay in the chopper! I'll get out, cuff him and then throw him in the cage. But watch his girlfriend, she'll come after you both."

Harry jumped out to cuff Will. Will took a swing at Harry. Harry ducked and then punched him square on the chin, knocking him to the ground.

The twins watched in disbelief. "Oh, my god, should we go help him, Sam?" Kyle asked.

"No," Sam said. "Harry can take care of himself. Watch this—it'll be a good lesson for you."

The twins opened the door and ran to help Harry.

"Get him, Kyle. Kick his cyborg butt!" Kate said. Kate ran after the girl.

"No, get back in the chopper and lock yourself in the cage," Harry said. "Do it now, before they kill you!"

Will jumped up and came at Harry, while his girlfriend grabbed each of the twins by their collar and dragged them down the street. They struggled to get loose when Harry flew in front of her and kicked out her legs. She let go of them. Then Kyle and Kate ran to the chopper and locked themselves in the cage.

Harry said, "So you want to play hardball, eh, kid?

"Yeah, sucker, fooled you!" he replied.

"And I think you had something to do with Carlita dying. Did you kill her?" Harry then shot Will and his girlfriend in the chest with laser bolts. They both dropped to the ground and gasped for air like fish out of water. But they were only stunned.

Harry laughed but Will jumped up and punched Harry in the mouth. Then the girl jumped on his back. Harry was twisting around and trying to shake her off his back when Carlita flew in and landed. "You got this, Harry. I got an alert my car was stolen."

"Grab crazy Karen, would you?" Harry said.

"Don't mind if I do!" Carlita grabbed the girl, slammed her on the ground, and kicked her in the stomach. "That was my car you stole!" However, this didn't faze the girl. She jumped right up and did a swinging ninja kick to Carlita's face, which knocked Carlita down. Carlita jumped up, swung around, swiped out the girl's legs with hers and stepped on her head, pinning her to the ground.

Harry then grabbed Will and threw him at Carlita. She threw him to the ground and she stepped on his head, so she had them both pinned to the ground. She asked Will, "Did you kill me?"

Both youngsters broke loose, popped up to their feet, and Will said, "You bet! What are you going to do about it?"

Carlita chuckled, winked at Harry and spun around with a ninja kick to Will's stomach, which sent him flying toward Harry. In return, Harry swung around with his own ninja kick to the face, and Will was down on the ground.

"For starters, I want to see you eliminated or spending the rest of your days in the cyborg supermax prison," said Carlita.

Will bounced up and shot Harry and Carlita with his own laser bolt, which stunned them momentarily.

Carlita engaged her left-arm rocket launcher and shot him in the face, sending him flying backward and into his girlfriend's arms. It burnt the skin off half his face and exposed his cyborg metal head.

Will and Karen flew off. Both Harry and Carlita regained their composure.

"Nice one, Carlita. First time I've seen your new upgraded technology," Harry said.

"Yeah, not bad for a princess," Carlita said as she winked at Harry.

"Oh my god, you guys, are you okay?" Kate asked. Harry walked toward the chopper, and Carlita opened the door to the Roadster. They blew a kiss at each other.

"I thought you said you had this, Harry," Carlita said.

"I did until you came along," Harry said.

"Really, I just saved you from a beat-down!"

"Okay, honey. You're right. Thank you for saving me; I am forever grateful," Harry said.

"Wow, that was cool seeing your rocket launcher! How the heck did you guys learn to fight like that?" Kyle asked. "You were throwing bolts of lightning at each other."

"Bond, James Bond." Harry laughed.

"Cyborgs come with many tools such as the bolt but they have limitations. The bolt works on people but only stuns cyborgs," Carlita said.

"So that's it? Will and his girlfriend get away after stealing her cool car?"

"Yes, I'm afraid so. He is a slippery one. He is baiting us to get to you both," Harry said. "And I'll do my best not to let that happen. If I could have gotten them in the cage then they would be trapped. But that is really hard to do."

"Okay guys, I'm going to run along and bring the car back," Carlita said. "See you all later."

Carlita stepped into the convertible Roadster and sped off with squealing tires. White smoke rose into the air accompanied by the smell of burning rubber. After two seconds the car reached one-hundred miles per hour and the thermal launchers kicked in. The car lifted off and soared upward at two-hundred miles per hour, leaving a white steam cloud tailing behind. Orange flames popped out of the burners as the car disappeared into the blue sky. The twins and Harry climbed into the chopper.

"I think I want to go with Carlita," Kate said.

"Too late, kid!" Harry said.

"So, who exactly are you, Sam?" Kyle asked.

"I'm the new sheriff in town," Sam barked. "I'm bigger and meaner than most cops, so watch out."

"Hey, dude," Kyle said, "what's with the attitude? We're just kids."

"Just kids, not spies?" Sam said. "I'm a cop, and the attitude goes with the territory."

"Of course we're not spies," Kyle said.

"Yeah, we don't know what you're talking about. Maybe you're taking this authority thing too far," Kate added.

"Maybe so, little lady," Sam replied, "but there's something you should know about this bad boy. I have six hundred horsepower and can chase down any trouble-maker. I also can fly up to four hundred miles an hour. I can carry six kids in the cage. Maybe I should leave you both in the cage since that's where kids belong."

"No, thanks Sam." Kyle snickered. "That's quite all right."

Sam lifted off, and they were all back at the heliport a few minutes later. Everyone exited the chopper.

"Why is Sam being so mean to us?" Kyle asked.

"Past problems with Will and his gang," Harry said. "Don't worry about it."

"A problem?" Kyle asked.

"Will is always getting the upper hand, as you just saw," Harry said.

"Will has a blown chip in his cyborg motherboard which we think makes him crazy," Harry warned. "Maybe an operation would fix it but he isn't going to let that happen. So he must go to the supermax prison for life or be eliminated. Your next stage is with the Muscle Men at

Lake Tahoe. I need to see how they're progressing with logging for our new top-secret base. Want to have some real fun and take a spin up to Tahoe?"

MUSCLE MEN

We terminate bullies!

"Sounds good to me," Kate replied.

"Yeah," Kyle agreed. "Sounds like fun."

Harry clenched each hand into a fist and then released them. He put his fingers together and cracked his knuckles, which disengaged his fingers. Then he cracked his knuckles three times really fast and extended his arms overhead. Each hand transformed into a large spinning rotor blade.

The twins' jaws went slack, and Kate said, "Oh, my god, Kyle, it's superhero time!"

Harry bent over at the waist. "Kyle, climb onto my back, and put your legs around my waist and your arms around my neck. Kate, climb on behind Kyle and put your arms around him and your legs around my stomach. Just a reminder, hold on tight or die!" Harry reached his arms forward as they took off. The twins shouted with excitement. After a few minutes of flying, Kate hollered, "It's so awesome to be flying on Harry's back!" They soared over the mountain peaks.

A short while later, Lake Tahoe came into view in the distance with its glimmering blue water surrounded by snow-capped mountains. The lake was full of activity; boats and waterskiers were zipping around.

"Wow, what a gorgeous lake," Kyle said. "I had no idea it was so big and blue." They zoomed over the tree-tops. "Isn't this a sick way to travel, with the wind in our faces?"

"Yeah," Kate said. "Just don't fall off!"

Harry began his descent toward the lake, and landed in a clearing in the woods. The buzz of chainsaws filled the air. They heard someone yell, "Timber!" Harry's hand rotors retracted, and his hands reappeared. The twins slid off his back.

"Watch out, kids," Harry said. "'Timber!' is the warning the guys give when trees are being dropped from the choppers or when the loggers are felling trees."

As the kids watched the choppers bring in trees, Kate tried to talk over the sound of the helicopters and the logging trucks. "Who's that praying mantis flying toward us? He's enormous! Is he from South America too?"

"No, not South America," Harry said. "He's a pretty cool dude when you get to know him. His name is

Muscle, and he's a muscle of a machine. Muscle grew up in Austria when times were hard there for young praying mantises. He moved to the United States and became an android, which didn't work so well in the beginning. But now he's found his true identity."

Muscle landed nearby in a clearing surrounded by huge stacks of felled trees.

"Hey, Muscle. How's it going?" Harry asked.

"Just fine," he said in his thick Austrian accent. We should have the area cleared soon for your new base, Harry," Muscle said.

"I want to introduce you to Kate and Kyle. They're training to be superheroes."

"Glad to meet you, kids. How's the training going?" Muscle asked. He leaned over and offered his green front leg for a hand slap.

"Amazing, Muscle," Kate said. "What big hands you have, and your voice sounds so familiar."

"Yeah, I get that all the time. I think it's my accent. Check this out." Muscle suddenly morphed into the Skycrane chopper. His body shook as his tail snapped into the tail rotor. Each leg was extended to ten feet long. His feet became tires as each leg molded into green steel. His face transformed into the cockpit, with each eye becoming a cockpit seat. Muscle glistened in the sizzling sun, his long, lean body of hardened orange steel towering over the twins.

"This is unbelievable!" Kyle shouted.

"Wow, completely amazing. That's one tough-looking dude," Kate gushed, pushing Kyle with excitement.

"This incredible helicopter was designed after my long, lean, muscular body and my ability to carry heavy loads," Muscle bragged. "I can carry twice my body weight—25,000—pounds, which is more than any other chopper in the world can carry." He brought his tentacle-like rotors down for a muscle-man flex. "Think of me as a *terminator* of sorts, especially when it comes to fire. I can fill my belly full of water and knock out fires in an instant!"

"Muscle, you're a beast. I want to be a Skycrane pilot!" Kyle exclaimed.

"So this is going to be your new base, Harry?" Kate asked, scanning an area cleared of trees.

"Yes," he said. "It's time we moved from our current location—it's too exposed. Will and his cyborg bullies from around the world won't find us here near Lake Tahoe. Who would think to look here? We have to try to stay one step ahead of them. They're after us as much as we're after them."

"Today our mission is trees," Muscle said. "Tomorrow, who knows? Maybe we'll save the world. So, kids, you want to help me pick up some big trees?"

"Heck, yeah!" Kyle replied.

"Then climb aboard," Muscle said. "We won't be long, Harry."

"Good," Harry said, stretching his arms above his head. "I'll take a little catnap while you're gone."

Muscle's cockpit was high off the ground. The twins climbed up the ladder from the fuselage into the cockpit and strapped themselves in. Muscle's eyes transformed into a bubble windshield. A bubble windshield provides space for the pilot's head and gives better visibility to look down at the ground.

"Kyle, start the engine," Muscle said.

Kyle flicked the key, and the engine rumbled to life. "Now pull up on the collective, steady the cyclic, and get us airborne, kid." He waited while Kyle did as instructed. "Harry has taught you well, I see."

"Oh, yeah, but Kate and I are fast learners too, and it helps that we have our empowering flight jackets," Kyle said.

They lifted off and flew deep into the forest, where loggers were felling trees in the distance as a one hundred foot choker cable trailed beneath the chopper. Kyle circled and hovered over a pile of large trees that were ready to be hauled away.

"Kyle," Muscle said, "steady the chopper while Kate and I work the cable and choker harness for the trees."

"The ground crew has signaled, and the trees are secure," Kate said after a few minutes.

"Okay, Kyle," Muscle said. "Give it some throttle and ease up on the collective. Don't go crazy."

Kyle pictured the throttle on Carlita's motorcycle and grinned widely. "I think we've got a heavy load," he said. "I can feel the chopper stressing under the weight of the trees."

Muscle groaned. "Let's get to the drop zone quickly."

They flew near the drop zone and circled into position. "Kyle," Muscle said, "the blue button on the cyclic stick will release the trees, but wait until I tell you."

Will flew in undetected with his own hand rotors and waited on top of a tree for the right moment to strike. He watched Kyle move the trees in a clearing not far from Harry. They were about one hundred feet off the ground when he slammed into the chopper, shocking Kyle. Kyle nervously released the load too soon, not noticing Harry in the path of the falling trees.

"Not yet, Kyle!" Muscle yelled.

"Oh, my god!" Kate winced.

Harry was lying against a large log and appeared to be napping. His hat was tilted down over his eyes. His legs were crossed, and his hands were folded over his belly. He had headphones on, so he couldn't hear Muscle and the twins coming. Will's plan was to crush Harry with the falling trees and then attack Kate and Kyle.

"Harry might get smashed if he doesn't wake up!" Kyle exclaimed.

"Timber!" Kate shouted through the loudspeaker.

Harry opened one eyelid, and saw the silhouette of trees falling toward him through the glaring sun. He rolled to his left as a huge tree crashed to the ground with a thunderous thump. A dust cloud rose up, and he rolled to the right as another huge tree slammed down within inches of him. Harry jumped to his feet and stumbled around, looking confused. He looked up at Muscle and waved his arms.

"What the heck?" Harry yelled.

Kyle called out over the loudspeaker, "Are you okay, Harry? Will smashed into the chopper and is trying to kill us."

Will landed and picked up a giant, long tree and slammed it to the ground, missing Harry by inches.

Harry flew into him pinning him to the ground. He rabbit-punched Will in the chest and face and then threw him into the air where he then bounced off the helicopter and back to the ground. They both picked up large trees and swung them like baseball bats at each other. Clouds of dust rose from all the thumping. When the dust settled,

Will and Harry stood their ground with fists raised when Kyle announced "Timber!" on the loudspeaker and a log was released and crushed. Will tossed the log aside and flew off.

Muscle landed, and the twins rejoined Harry.

"That was close, Harry. I thought he just wanted us but he wants you too," Kyle said.

"Yes, but to get to you, he must go through me," Harry said.

"Wow, Harry, that was quite some fight. Are you okay?" Kate asked. "Sorry we couldn't do more."

"No worries, there will be plenty more chances. He is like a pesky mosquito that won't go away until he dies." Harry pointed to a yellow helicopter with twin rotors flying their way. "Check out Vertical Viktor coming in with a bundle of trees. He's another heavy-duty powerlifter."

Vertical Viktor released his trees, which made loud thuds and shook the ground. He landed in a clearing for the choppers, and everyone shuffled over to chat with him. Although Viktor was getting old, he had a youthful energy that never seemed to end, and he was built like a rock star. Muscle and Viktor had known each other since they were built. They each raised their rotors to slap each other and give each other a warm greeting.

"Hey, you're working too hard, Viktor. Give it a rest!" Harry said. "I brought some kids by—Kate and Kyle."

Viktor looked their way. "What was all the commotion?"

"Will tried to get to the twins again," Harry said.

"Ah, I see. We need to organize a game plan for his demise. Although Muscle and I have moved a lot of trees today, tell us what we need to do. Even though we have many more to move by the end of the day, I'm worried that we won't finish in time," Vicktor said.

"Don't worry about it. Now that Will has found this location, it's not going to work," Harry said.

"Okay then," Muscle said. "We'll still get it done. And that's why me and Viktor the Victorious will find a way to terminate him. What if we mince him in our rotor blades?"

"No, he will jam your blades and make you crash. He is as tough as they come," Harry said.

Viktor leaned over, smiled and tapped his rotor against Muscle's. "Not to brag, but I can power-lift twenty thousand pounds of trees in one lift with my four-thousand-horsepower engine which can terminate hate any day!"

"We know, but you're not tough enough to terminate Will. I'll need to figure out another solution. Time to get you're children home before Will kills you," Muscle said.

"We don't want to go home. Our superhero training is just getting started. Pleeeease, Harry," Kate begged.

"Well, don't make me regret this. You want to have some real fun and fly right into Lake Tahoe?"

"Yeah!" Kate exclaimed.

"Brilliant! You bet! How are we going to dry off? We don't have any towels," Kyle said.

"Not to worry. You'll be blown dry in no time while we fly back to base. Bye, Viktor. See ya, Muscle," Harry said.

"See ya later," Viktor said.

"Hasta la vista, baby," Muscle added.

Harry's hands extended into rotors. The kids climbed onto his back, and Harry took off. They were soaring over Lake Tahoe when Harry said, "Hold on tight and hold your breath!" They entered the water and exited after a few seconds.

"Wow!" The twins yelled.

They flew back home, paralleling the highway.

Kate cheered, "Man, Harry, this is so awesome!"

"This has to be the most fantastic ride ever," Kyle said. "Can we do it again?"

"Maybe another time. We're on a schedule."

"Hey, Kate," Kyle said, "I can see the city down there. The cars on the highway look so small."

"Yeah, they do. This sure beats driving," Kate said.

Fiona and Poo Daddy

Bullies always pay the price!

After they landed at the heliport, Harry said, "Don't you think your folks are worried?"

"No, we still have time. It's not dark yet, although the day is going by quickly. What do you have in mind next?" Kate said.

"Okay, this next stop is not actual crime fighting, but fire fighting. I need to pay a visit to Chuck and his helicopter Fiona. They are undercover spies and act as if they're firefighters. However, they are on the lookout for Will and his gang of troublemakers. We almost lost Chuck and Fiona a year ago when they crashed into a lake. Fiona had been picking up water while fighting a fire. The fire was started by Will and his gang of bullies. So Chuck might not be terribly excited to see kids so soon."

"Fiona survived?" Kyle said.

"Yes, but she required major reconstructive surgery," Harry explained. "And she is a fine android now. Although Chuck died from his injuries, he was rebuilt into a cyborg."

Harry checked his watch and thoughtfully said, "Let's play it by ear and see how this goes. We might not stay long,"

The twins climbed back onto Harry again. He spun them up and over the mountaintops to an air-attack base nestled in a valley.

Chuck gave a wave, and Harry glided in to land near several firefighting choppers.

"We need our own superhero hand rotors to make our friends jealous," Kate said.

Kyle grinned. "Oh, man, that would be the best."

"Here we are," Harry said. "Home of the aerial fire-fighting choppers. There's Chuck." He pointed to a big guy with large forearms and a potbelly. "Hey, Chuck!" Harry shouted through the gate. "Can we come in?"

"Sure, Harry." Chuck walked over and opened the gate. "It's been a while. How have you been?"

Chuck extended his hand to shake.

Harry pointed to Kate and Kyle. "I have these children with me and thought I'd give them a lesson on how you came in contact with Will and fire."

"Who are these children, Harry? Should they be here?"

"Oh, they are my new protégés," Harry said.

"And you and Fiona are part of our elite team, so I felt they should learn from the best."

"Great-looking chopper." Kyle said.

"Yes," Chuck said, his pudgy face gleaming with pride as he snapped his suspenders. They matched Fiona's color scheme. "She's a fine machine. Doesn't she just shine? I gave her a new wax job today, and she's as red as the sun. Climb on in. I treat her like she's my sweetheart, with loving care. You know how sensitive girls can be."

"Oh, yeah," Kyle said, and rolled his eyes at Kate.

"She sure does sparkle," Kate said. "Looks like you're real proud of her, Chuck." She poked her head inside and saw a bear sitting in the cockpit. "On my god, its a *BEAR!*"

"Yup, that's Poo Daddy," Harry said. "No need to be afraid unless you upset him. He's quite friendly. And he's proved to be one of our best when it comes to helping eliminate bullies and fighting the fires they start. He's even more of a badass bear when it comes to bullies, and he's been known to shred cyborgs to pieces."

"Hi, kids," Poo Daddy muttered.

"Hi, Poo Daddy," Kyle said. "Are you a cyborg too?"

"No, I'm an android! And I'm one of the meanest! Hey Harry, are they bear bait?" He laughed as he licked his chops.

"What big brown eyes, sharp white teeth, and long claws you have," Kate said. "Oh, and your furry barrel chest really shows off your gold chain necklace nicely."

"Nice shades, too," Kyle said.

"Yeah, and sharp teeth to eat you with," Poo Daddy said.

"Seems Poo Daddy is a little testy," Kate said.

Chuck turned and whispered, "Well, maybe that's because Poo Daddy became an orphan when his mother was bullied, chased, and finally killed by a hunter. He's still pretty upset and rightly so. He was wandering aimlessly through the woods and trying to find somewhere to hide from the hunter when he crawled into a chopper and fell asleep. The chopper's pilots were out searching for the careless hunters who had started the fire. Poo Daddy left quite a mess of bear poop in the chopper before he died. So the pilots gave him the name Poo Daddy when he was rebuilt into an android."

While Harry began talking to Chuck, Kyle leaned into Poo Daddy and whispered, "I feel for you. Kate and I have been bullied plenty at our school."

"Is that how you got those black eyes?" Poo Daddy asked.

"Yes, Will and his girlfriend got us pretty good and broke our toy helicopters," Kyle said.

"Wow, maybe I'll break him in half like he broke your toys."

"That would be great, please do," Kate said. "By any chance, have you seen Harry's time machine? Please tell us you have?"

"Yeah, kid," Poo Daddy said. "What do you want to know!"

Fiona piped up. "Mind if I take over?"

"Go right ahead, sister," Poo Daddy replied.

Before Fiona could answer, "I just received a call from dispatch in my earpiece. Will and his gang blew up your new base at Lake Tahoe. The forest is on fire, and the flames have spread to the casinos. Fiona and I need to go." He turned to Harry. "Do you want to come and help and maybe take out Will if there is a chance?"

Kate butted in, "Can we come?"

"The twins aren't ready for this, are they Harry?"

"I can understand if you don't want us to come." Kate pouted a little as she kicked at the ground.

"Well, this is one way to make them ready," Harry said.

Chuck exhaled as he looked at Harry. "Okay, you can come, but don't touch anything!"

Kyle tugged on Kate's hair. "Yeah, Kate, no brain farts. Don't do anything *stupid,* dork!" He snapped the elastic band on her underpants.

"Ow! Dang it, Kyle!"

"I owed you one."

Chuck and Harry laughed.

Kate sat next to Chuck, while Kyle and Harry took seats in the back. "Is everyone buckled in?" asked Chuck, speaking through his headset microphone. Everyone gave him the thumbs up. How about you, Poo Daddy? Are you with us, buddy? While the others had been talking, Poo Daddy had climbed into his own android chopper, the Copter Cub. He was ready for action.

"Ten-four," Poo Daddy said. "I'm locked in and ready when you are."

With a turn of the key, Fiona's engine rumbled and started with a bang. The helicopter vibrated as the rotor sliced through the air, creating a windstorm.

"I'm warmed up," Fiona said. "Let's roll."

"Great," Chuck said. "I'll roll on more throttle and get us airborne."

"I see smoke off on the horizon," Kyle said, pointing.

Chuck nodded. "That's the fire. Let's keep an eye out for more choppers. We don't want to fly into any of them. With all the smoke, it's going to get pretty crazy up here. I need you all to keep your eyes peeled."

They entered clouds of thick gray smoke as they got closer to the fire.

"This fire is out of control!" Harry yelled.

"Yeah!" Kyle shouted. "It's beginning to swallow up the town of Lake Tahoe! The flames look like they're a hundred feet high."

"It looks like a dragon on a rampage!" Kate exclaimed.

"Yup," Chuck said. "It's time to slay the beast. We don't have much time before the whole town is engulfed in flames. I'm going to swing over to the lake and pick up a load of water. It only takes about sixty seconds to fill up the bucket. We will hover ten feet above the lake while the bucket fills up." They watched water skiers ski by while they waited." Chuck turned to Kate. "Remember, don't touch anything."

"Okay!" Fiona cried. "The bucket is full!"

"Ten-four," Chuck replied.

As they began to lift off, Fiona's heavy load started to stress the engine, and the rotor made more of a chopping sound.

"Hurry up and get to the fire, Chuck," Fiona said, "My belly is about to burst." And she burped.

"I hear you, girl," Chuck said. "We'll be there in a couple of minutes." As they approached the fire, Chuck blurted out, "Kate, you see the red button on the cyclic stick?"

"Yes," she said, and smiled.

"It opens the fire bucket and dumps water on the flames."

Kate was surprised that Chuck was letting her help. "Got it, Chuck," she said. "What does the yellow button do?"

"Don't touch that button," Chuck said. "That'll release the cable with the bucket."

They swooped low over the flames for a water drop. Blondy's Princess Palace and Casino was engulfed in flames. People were standing outside and watching as Muscle and Viktor rotated through with water drops.

"Okay," Chuck said. "Let it rain, girl."

Kate released the water.

"Bull's-eye, Kate!" Harry said. "That water drop snuffed out the fire on the roof of the casino."

They continued to gather and drop water. After about ten water drops, everything seemed to be going smoothly until Poo Daddy radioed in a panic. "Will flew into Muscle's water bucket using his hand rotors and started swinging the bucket around so it would catch and tangle in your rotor blade."

"Good eye, Poo Daddy," Chuck responded. "I'll pull up so Muscle can go underneath us. Radio Muscle and let him know we're here."

"Up we go," Chuck said, pulling back on the stick. This pointed the nose of the chopper up, and Muscle flew beneath them. But his rotor became entangled in the cable that held the fire bucket, and both helicopters spun out of control toward the ground. Everyone freaked out as Chuck tried to maintain control of the helicopter.

"This isn't working!" Chuck shouted. "What should we do, Harry?"

"Does anyone see Will?" Harry asked.

"No," Muscle said.

"Do something quick before we hit the ground!" Fiona yelled.

"Hurry!" Muscle hollered.

"Kate!" Poo Daddy called out. "Push the yellow button on the stick to release the cable and the bucket!"

Kate fumbled with the button, her fingers slipping off it. She finally got her thumb on it and released the bucket and the fifty-foot cable.

"That's using your thumb, Kate!" Chuck said, as he regained control of the helicopter and radioed Muscle. "Is everything okay on your end, Muscle?"

"No! The bucket hit the Copter Cub and became tangled in the rotor. Poo Daddy is going to crash."

Just then, Poo Daddy jumped out of the chopper. He engaged his hand rotors and flew to the ground. Everyone watched the chopper crash to the ground.

"Is Poo Daddy okay down there by himself, fully exposed to Will and his gang?" Kyle asked. "And why couldn't the chopper fly itself to the ground?"

"The Copter Cub did not get the final android moth-erboard it needed to prevent the crash. And he can look after himself," Chuck said. "He will bait Will like he bait's you."

"I hope you are right about that," Kyle said. Will flew by them and landed next to the crumpled Copter Cub.

Fiona stopped and hovered and watched to see what transpired.

"Will and Poo Daddy have been enemies since he was a cub. Will's father was the hunter that killed Poo

Daddy's mother," Chuck said. "Poo Daddy has always been on the lookout for Will. He has wandered the woods searching for him and his band of thugs, who are elusive most of the time. Will has no idea that he is about to get a bear beat down."

"Break him in half!" Kate shouted through the loudspeaker.

Poo Daddy and Will saw each other and squared off. "Hey bear, I hear you're looking for me!"

"Not just you but your parents who killed my mom!"

"You have to go through me to get to my parents!"

Poo Daddy stood up on his hind legs and punched Will in the face with rabbit punches. Before Will had any time to react from his daze, he grabbed him by the neck with his teeth and shook him around like a rag doll and tossed him onto his crumpled Cub chopper. Will lay there, pretending to be dead. When Poo Daddy walked over to check on him, Will launched himself at the bear. They both tumbled to the ground, Will on top of him. He was straddling Poo Daddy's body and had his hands on Poo Daddy's neck.

"We should help him," Kate said.

"Not yet—only when Poo Daddy gives the sign," Chuck said. "Which is a thumbs down."

"He's going to go bear crazy right about now. Watch this," Harry said.

Poo Daddy did a Ninja flip backwards and landed on Will. He picked Will up in a bear hug and tried to squeeze the life out of him. But Will was strong. He broke free and flew off. Poo Daddy gave a thumbs up and flew up with his hand rotors and joined everyone in the chopper.

"Nice job," Kyle said

"Not nice enough. I can't beat the power out of him, because he is so strong. But one day, I'll figure out how to short-circuit him."

Chuck announced, "We'll head back because we don't have a bucket anymore. I'll leave it up to you and the boys to mop up what's left of the fire."

"Ten-four. Consider the fire *terminated*," Muscle said.

Fiona landed back at their air-attack base.

Kyle shook his head. "That has to be the most exciting helicopter job there is, Harry."

"One of the most demanding jobs, too," Harry said. "And that probably wasn't quite the superhero training you were expecting."

"Could we have died?" Kyle asked.

"Heck, yeah," Harry said. "Still think you want to be a superhero?"

"Sure we do," Kyle said. "Especially if we can learn to fight like Poo Daddy."

They said their goodbyes, and flew back to base.

Captain Calypso

Never stay defeated!

Harry rubbed his chin as he walked down the warm tarmac with the twins following. He stopped in front of a helicopter.

"Have either of you been to the Gulf Coast?" he asked.

The kids shook their heads.

"I'll show you the next chopper in this superhero lesson on how dolphins immobilize bad guys."

"Excellent!" Kyle exclaimed. "We love dolphins."

"Okay," Harry said. "Let's take a spin out to the Dolphin Guard facility on the Gulf Coast to see if there's any news about the dolphin training that's taking place there. It's quite far away, so let's take my really—fast helicopter, Turbo."

"How fast is Turbo?" Kyle asked.

"I'm faster than fast!" Turbo stuttered. "There ain't an android helicopter f-faster than me! I'm j-j-jet engine fast."

"He tends to stutter when he gets excited." Harry said.

Harry fired up Turbo as Kate jumped into the front seat and Kyle jumped into the back. Kate scanned the dash and noticed that the gauges and controls weren't much different than the ones in the other choppers.

"I hope you guys are ready for the r-ride of a lifetime," Turbo called out.

"Stop bragging, Turbo," Harry said. "You're going to scare them."

"We love speed, don't we, Kyle?"

Kyle high-fived Kate and smiled.

"Well, then, buckle up and get ready to rock!" Turbo shouted. "Once the turbos kick in, we'll go faster than fast. It'll get loud, so make sure your headsets are on and working."

"Are we warmed up, Turbo?" Harry asked. The chopper was vibrating unlike the others. It felt like they had extreme power under their seats.

"Yes, I'm fired up and ready to blast off."

"Hold on, kids," Harry said. "Here we go."

They grabbed the sides of their seats and blasted off toward the Gulf Coast. Their bodies sank into the seats as the chopper accelerated.

"Hey, Harry," Turbo said, "are you ready to put the scare in the twins?"

"Go for it, Turbo, but easy on the scare."

As soon as Harry said this, the turbo-charged engine kicked in, and they took off like a shooting star.

"Wow, I never imagined going this fast before," Kate said, her face stretched tight.

"It won't be long till we're on the Gulf Coast," Harry said. "Would you like to steer the chopper, Kate?"

"Yes!"

"Okay, take hold of the cyclic stick and keep your eyes straight ahead," Harry instructed. "Use that mountaintop about twenty miles away as a reference point, and steer the chopper toward it but not into it." Harry chuckled.

"This is too easy," Kate said. "Helicopters aren't so hard to fly—I mean a fourth grader can do it. Hey, what's this lever that says TT?"

"It's nothing," Harry said. "Now put your foot on the pedals and push each one to keep us flying in a straight line."

Harry watched as Kate pressed on the pedals. "Keep the mountaintop in sight," he continued. "Push a little harder on the left pedal and a little more on the right. Pull the cyclic back and raise the nose." Kate pulled too hard on the cyclic, and the nose went straight up, and the emergency horn came on. The helicopter stalled and the motor quit and began to fall to the ground.

"Hey Turbo, a little help here," Kate said.

"Sorry, as an android there is only so much I can do. You're on your own, kid."

As the nose came straight up, the helicopter rolled over backwards. The chopper fell like a rock through the sky toward the ground. Harry grabbed the controls. He was able to get the chopper upright but could not get it started. Harry tried persistently, turning the key over and over.

"Come on Turbo–you need to help!" Harry said.

"I'm running diagnostics as we speak. A circuit board has malfunctioned and needs rebooting."

"What do we do?" Harry asked.

"Press hard on both pedals and jerk the collective up right now. That should reboot us," Turbo said. Harry did as Turbo said. The power came back on, and they were flying again.

"Nice flying, Harry," Kyle said.

"No problem," Harry said, wiping the sweat off his brow. "Just need to remember your ABCs."

"Point well taken," Kyle said. "That's the first time I've seen you sweat, Harry."

"Hey, we're getting close to the Mississippi Gulf Coast. You should be able to see the water sparkling off in the distance. I'll fly over the dolphins and land nearby."

"I see pretty beaches," Kate said. "I want to go for a swim."

"Go for it, Kate," Kyle said. "Jump in and scare the fish. You're the wild one."

"Yes, I am the wild one but I'll pass on scaring the fish today."

Harry pointed out the window. "The Mississippi Gulf Coast is one of the places where dolphins train to become helicopters. We'll land near the Oceanarium, next to the Dolphin Guard headquarters."

After they landed, the twins bolted out of the chopper, running over to the dolphins in their holding pens. The smell of the salty ocean breeze surrounded them.

Kate shook her head. "Dolphins turning into helicopters?" Dolphins splashed through the water in the distance.

"Did you know some dolphins can fly but not all? They require specialized training."

"What happens to the dolphins that can't fly?" Kyle asked.

"Do they go to SeaWorld and live a life of luxury?" Kate joked.

The twins broke into laughter again. Harry grinned. "Ha, ha. Some do, and the ones that make it are honored to perform at SeaWorld due to the competitive selection process. The others are selected to join the Navy SEALs and enter training for the MK6 underwater surveillance program. They spy on troublemakers, with cameras. Once they locate one, they shoot him in the butt with their dart guns."

Kyle laughed. "Get out!" he said. "How do they pull the trigger?"

"It helps that they are androids. They squeeze it with their teeth," Harry replied. "And if that doesn't work, they chew through the swimmer's air hose. With no air, the troublemaker swims to the surface like there's no tomorrow."

"Androids rule!" Kyle said.

Harry pointed to the leader of the dolphins. "Check out Captain Calypso, the instructor. She's a true southern belle and loves to fly. See her jumping high out of the water, doing flips? She's a lady who likes to strut her stuff. Watch out for her big splash."

The twins jumped back to avoid getting wet. But they weren't quick enough and got splashed in their faces. They rubbed their lips with the back of their hands to get rid of the saltwater taste.

"Why are all the student dolphins wearing headsets and sunglasses?" Kyle asked.

"Take a guess," Harry said.

"Are they pilots?" Kate asked.

"Not just pilots, but android choppers."

"No way!" Kate shouted "Dolphins can't fly!"

Harry smiled. "These ones can because they're androids. They've been specially trained like no others. Dolphins can be trained to do a lot of things. In fact, they're the only animals that can read."

"Seriously? Read like us?" Kate asks.

"Yes, recent research has discovered their unique ability to read. As unbelievable as it sounds, it's true."

Kate whispered to Kyle, "Let's test Calypso on her reading ability to see if Harry's pulling our leg."

"Calypso has rescued many people stranded on rooftops during hurricanes and floods, and many people on sinking boats," Harry said.

Calypso swam up and popped her head out of the water. "I do declare, if it ain't—Prince Charming! Tell me it's not so. What brings you to the Gulf, so far from home?"

Calypso was a slender, smart bottlenose dolphin who had been orphaned shortly after she was born. Her lean body glistened in the sun as the water rolled off her skin. The Navy SEALs had adopted her and made her into a fearless android.

"And She is in charge of this secret unit. Calypso is not just another superhero but a grand master," Harry said.

"Hey, kids, you know we have a lot of fun saving people. It's like a bonding experience. Let me guess how you got those black eyes. A bully from your school?"

"Not just any bully but Will," Kyle said.

"Shame on him!" Calypso said.

"Why are bubbles of air coming to the surface as you talk?" Kate asked.

Calypso looked embarrassed. "Those are fart bubbles from when I talk."

Kate laughed and poked Kyle, "Sounds like my brother in the bathtub."

"Do you miss the MK6 program?" Kate asked.

"It was great fun in years past, but it's too much excitement for this old Southern belle," Calypso said, batting her eyelashes. "Although, if you ever decide to challenge authority—and what kid doesn't—you might feel the sting of my dart when you least expect it."

Harry laughed and poked Kate.

Kate rolled her eyes at Kyle. "Yeah, right!"

"But protecting and saving people—that's my real passion," Calypso said.

"So what you're saying is that you'd do this even if it weren't your job?" Kyle said.

"Yes, you might say that. In fact, dolphins were saving people long before we became helicopters."

"Calypso, tell me something," Kate said. "Would you rather be free to swim in the ocean or rescue people?"

"I get bored just swimming around all the time," Calypso said. "Rescuing people gives me a sense of pride. Don't get me wrong. I love to do tricks and make huge splashes like my friends. But we need to find a balance between work and play. Would you like to see a video clip of our rescues from Hurricane Maria?"

Kate nodded. "Please show us, Calypso."

"I suppose you have your phone handy?" Kyle asked.

"I sure do," Calypso said. "We record the dolphins and then play the footage back to them to help improve their flying techniques."

As Calypso started the video on her phone and blue-toothed it to a big screen hanging on the wall., Kyle whispered to Kate, "This is a little weird—flying dolphins."

Kate whispered back, "Yeah, but this whole training is weird. It's like we're in some kind of animated movie."

Kyle pointed to the screen, where water was flooding the streets of Puerto Rico. "Check out those kids on that rooftop. The dolphin chopper arrives just in time with the basket."

"Were those gators I saw swimming around the roof-top?" Kate asked after the video clip ended.

"Yeah, you saw right," Calypso replied. "But what you didn't see was the gator that swallowed a little boy as the kids were lifted off the roof." She tossed her head back and laughed. Just kidding!"

"But three hungry gators did scamper onto the roof, snapping their jaws, as we left."

"Wow, that was close," Kyle said.

"We need to let Calypso get back to her training," Harry said, nudging the twins.

"Maybe Kyle and I could ride on Calypso's back before we go?" Kate asked eagerly.

Harry laughed. "Ride on her back! She's too busy, right, Calypso?"

"Well…let's consider it superhero training," Calypso said. "But we'll need to make it quick so I can get back to my students. Why don't you both climb onto my back and hold tight to my dorsal fin?"

"Kate, maybe you should fix your boot lace as it looks untied," Harry said.

"Okay, I'll get to it when we get back." Kate said.

Kate and Kyle climbed onto Calypso's back.

"Oh!" Kate said. "I feel another wild ride coming on."

They propelled through the water and jumped high into the air as Calypso morphed into a Dolphin Guard helicopter. Calypso snapped her tail. The vibration shot through her body to her head, transforming her tail into the tail rotor. Her side fins became wheels, and her dorsal fin extended like a periscope as it became the rotor. Her body transformed into the fuselage, and her head and nose morphed into the cockpit, with Kate in the pilot seat and Kyle as the co-pilot.

"Pretty cool, Calypso," Kyle said.

Just then, Calypso took a call on her Bluetooth headset. "A distress call is coming in from a family that their sailboat is sinking. Let's go pick them up—they're not far. We'll be there in a few minutes. Kate, Kyle, I want you guys to hoist them up with the basket. Do you see the boat?" Calypso asked.

After a few minutes of flying, they spotted a white and blue sailboat bobbing in the ocean. Waves were rolling over the boat, and a man was waving from the deck. It was a warm day and the sun was shining brightly but the water was chilly.

"It's right in front of us, being battered by the waves. Looks like it's just one man, and his boat will be underwater in minutes. We need to hurry. Are you ready with the basket, kids?"

"Yes," Kate called out. "We're lowering it as you speak." Then a white streak passed by. It passed by again in the other direction. It was Will doing a really fast fly-by.

The twins spoke into their wireless headsets as they lowered the basket to the man on the boat. He climbed in, and the twins hoisted him up. Suddenly, Will flew into the side of the helicopter and it jerked to the right. Kate tumbled thirty feet into the cold blue water, and white-capped waves rolled over her. The basket reached the chopper, and the man climbed inside. Kyle handed him a blanket. "Is it just you, mister?"

"I'm afraid so," he said. "I lost my wife and two kids. None of them could swim as the waves washed them into the ocean."

"I'm so sorry for your loss, mister. Should we try to find them?"

"No, they are gone. But let's save your sister," he said.

"Kate, are you alright? I just saw Will and he stuck his tongue out at me as he flew by." Kyle called into the headset. "You sure made a big splash." He laughed. "How's the water? Did it take your breath away?"

With her teeth chattering, Kate responded, "R-e-a-l f-u-n-n-y! Y-e-a-h, d-a-m-n c-o-l-d. But could you h-u-r-r-r-y with the b-a-s-s-s-s-k-e-t? It's s-o-o c-o-o-o-l-d." She swam over to the boat and held onto it. Waves rolled over her and the boat as the basket was lowered. The wind and waves spun the basket around, swinging it towards Kate and then out of reach. Her entire day flashed before her eyes as her near-death experience unfolded. *So this is superhero training?* she thought.

In her dreamlike state, she heard a voice. "Kate!" Kyle yelled. "Grab the basket and climb in, Kate!"

The basket swung around to Kate, but she couldn't quite reach it. Her bootlace was caught on the boat railing. She could only touch the basket with her fingertips as it slipped away, just out of her grasp. Then the boat sank, and Kate sank with it. She held up her arm as she slowly disappeared under the water. Her fingers wiggled slightly, and she gave a thumbs-up before she disappeared.

"Oh, my god, Calypso!" Kyle yelled frantically. "Kate went down with the boat."

"Any sign of her?"

"No!" Kyle said. "Only bubbles. I'm going in for her!"

"Yes, do what you need to do and save her, Kyle. Give her CPR if she isn't breathing. You know how to do CPR, right, Kyle? You need to bring her up quickly for that," Calypso said.

"Yes, we just learned how to do it in our health and fitness class." Kyle engaged the autopilot control and turned to the man. "Dude, you have to work the basket."

"No problemo, *amigo*," the man said. "Go save your sister, and I'll bring her up in the basket."

Kyle jumped into the freezing water and swam around to where the boat was. He dove down until he saw Kate's stretched-out body with her arms and hair pointing upwards. She didn't appear to be moving. He swam down and tried to jerk her foot free from the railing, but it wouldn't come loose. He dug his hand deep into his pants and pulled out a pocket knife to cut the lace. He struggled to get the blade to open and the knife slipped out of his hands. His heart sank as he watched it sink through the murky water into the dark abyss. He gave one last hard tug with all his strength on the boot and it broke free. He brought Kate to the surface. The man guided the basket to Kyle and he loaded Kate into it.

Calypso shouted. "Give her CPR, Kyle and don't give up until she starts breathing."

Kyle's eyes welled up with tears as he climbed half-way onto the basket and attempted to give Kate CPR. He pinched her nose and blew air into her mouth. Her chest expanded as Kyle blew into her mouth but she did not wake up. He blew again and nothing. Kyle was getting very tired and wanted to try again when a large wave washed over both of them taking Kyle with it. The man didn't see Kyle so he thought it best to bring Kate up. He hoisted Kate's body into the chopper within seconds. The man lifted her onto the chopper floor and proceeded to lower the basket to where he last saw Kyle. But he couldn't see Kyle through the rolling waves. Then he saw him floating in the frothy white water, face down and not moving. Then Will did a flyby and stuck out his tongue. He then mouthed *"Ha, ha, I killed them!"* He then flew off.

"Looks like Kyle drowned while trying to save Kate," he said to Calypso.

"Oh my god! I was afraid of that. He surely wore himself out trying to save his sister. I need to you fish his body out and bring him up. Then I need to get them into the cyber chamber while their bodies are still warm."

The man lowered himself down to the water and grabbed Kyle's arm and pulled him into the basket. They were both back in the chopper within seconds. Both kids were laid out on the floor of the chopper. He laid a blanket over them covering their heads. Time was running out fast for reconstruction.

Calypso radioed Harry and said, "We have a code blue!"

"I'm so sorry, Harry, the twins drowned. Will got to them: he must have known you weren't with us. Maybe somebody tipped him off."

"If so, then there is a spy amongst us," Harry said. "Maybe one of your students? They are at the age where they can be bullied into doing stupid things."

They landed back at the Oceanarium. Harry greeted Calypso and the man. "Hello, I am Helicopter Harry. Are you okay?"

"Si, I am fine. I am Enrique, and I am sorry for your loss." Harry pulled the blanket back from their heads, rubbed his eyes and then pulled the blanket back over their heads. Enrique was about forty years old, and as tall as Harry, with a tan complexion and black hair. He was wearing a white T-shirt, plaid shorts and sandals.

"It's all my fault," Harry said. "I shouldn't have let them out of my sight."

"What is done is done," Calypso said. "We must get them into the cyber chamber for reconstruction immediately. I alerted the technicians as we flew back. Are you okay, Harry?"

"Yes, I'm just a little taken aback. I'll be fine. Well, the twins get their wish to become cyborgs. We have only one hour before their bodies cool too much and we lose them forever," Harry said.

Harry shook Enrique's hand and said. "Thank you for your help. What were you doing out there?"

"I was on my way from Cuba to the States. The ocean became very rough and waves broke over my boat. I am forever grateful to the kids for saving my life."

"Can I call you a ride?" Harry asked.

"No, I have family in the area." He walked away.

Harry jumped in the chopper. They flew to a top-secret hospital and landed within minutes on the roof-top. Technicians in white coats took the twins and placed them onto stretchers. They were hurried into the cyber chamber to begin the process of being rebuilt into cyborgs. "Strip their clothes off!" Jackie, the technician yelled. "My team will take Kate, and Ted's team will take Kyle."

"Hurry, good people: we are short on time," Harry said.

After two hours of reconstruction, the twins were lying in beds next to each other in a dimly lit hospital room. The door creaked open and a technician walked in. She startled Harry, who had dozed off in the reclining chair. "Any movement yet?"

Harry snapped awake. "Nope, nothing."

"Okay then. We need to jump-start them with a charge to bring them back." She hooked up a machine and then plugged in the twins at the back of their heads like a phone charger. She turned up the juice and asked Harry, "Anything?"

"Not yet," Harry said.

She gave them a jolt but nothing happened. No sign of life. She jolted them again but nothing.

She opened their eyelids and shone a light into their eyes.

"Anything?" Harry asked.

She looked at Harry, shook her head and ran to the wall to press an alarm button. A team of technicians raced in with carts of machines. She opened the back of the kids' heads, which exposed circuit boards.

"Replace the chips and boards," one technician yelled out. "Wait a minute: this doesn't look right. Why is Kate's chip in Kyle and Kyle's chip in Kate? Did somebody switch them? Did anybody come in the room while you were here, Harry?"

"Uh...I'm not sure. I fell asleep. Wasn't there a guard at the door?"

"Yes, and he is gone." A look of horror swept across the technician's face. "He must have switchted them when you fell asleep."

"Will came in disguised as a guard, I bet," Harry said.

"Okay, ready to reboot," the technician said. And closed the back of their heads.

She rebooted the twins with a charge, and their eyes jolted open in a haunting way. Harry let out a gasp and took a step back. They both snapped up quickly in bed and looked at each other and then at Harry. They looked down at the hospital gowns they were wearing.

"What the?" Kate said.

"So are we dead or alive?" Kyle said.

"Both! Sorry, but you drowned out there. And now you guys are cyborgs. This was not part of the plan, kids." Harry handed each of them a mirror.

"Hey, we still have our black eyes," Kate said.

"Yes, and they will fade in a week or two. We want to keep you as human as possible."

"It's alright Harry. I got my wish," Kate said.

"You will have a lot of learning to do and it will take time before you are a fully functional cyborg and can fly with your hand rotors."

"Oh, my god!" Kyle yelled. So we have titanium under our skins and are indestructible like you, Harry!"

"I'm afraid so," Harry said.

"I don't remember much other than falling into the cold water, and going down with the boat. I struggled to loosen my bootlace from the railing but I ran out of breath. As everything went black I remembered you saying I had a loose lace that needed tightening," Kate said.

"I remember jerking your boot lace from the deck railing, bringing you to the surface, and loading you into the basket. And I gave you CPR a couple of times and then a big wave rolled over me, and it all went black," Kyle said. "I was so tired."

"Oh gross! Your lips were on my lips?"

"Yes, I'm afraid so, as gross as that was. I tried not to barf!" Kyle joked.

"Okay, nobody can ever know your lips were on mine. deal or no deal?"

"Deal, Kate, nobody knows but Harry and Calypso and maybe Enrique."

"Okay, moving right along. Quite the superhero experience you both had. Your new cyborg brains are rebooting with a new chip and circuitry, which will take time. However, your memories will be restored," Harry said. "As cyborgs, you are incredibly smart. You really don't have to go to school although you need the social aspect. And your brains have the equivalent of a college PhD in Nuclear Engineering. Because the Internet is in your cyborg brain, you have a plethora of knowledge at your instant disposal. Any math calculation you need to solve will be accomplished within seconds and without working it out on paper. This knowledge can help you build a spaceship or time travel. If kids ever bother you at school or call you dumb, ask them to calculate the algorithm of spaceships taking off and landing back in the same place. And then watch their eyes roll back into their heads. The world we live in revolves around algorithms, which most people don't understand. But you will do the calculation in seconds."

"Oh my god, this keeps getting better and better. I'm so glad the coin toss worked out, Kyle!" Kate said.

"Oh, yeah, this is super cool!"

"You will need to download the cyborg app for current updates. And it will make you both lethal. You will have laser bolts that fire from your fingers and exceptional fighting skills," Harry said. "And the bandage around your wrist.—that's tattoo that identifies you as one of ours. Take the bandage off." The twins removed the bandages.

"Wow, awesome!" Kyle said.

"Oh my god," Kate said. This is so cool."

"The tattoo is an identifier only. Sort of like a password. You're not going to show it off and it will blend into your skin color. You never show it to people and only to fellow cyborgs. If a bully does threaten you, then you walk away in the opposite direction. If the bully follows you and does not go away you are to smack him in the forehead with the palm of your hand. This will stun him and confuse him about why he was picking on you. You only use your superhero powers as a last resort against people. For instance, if you are ganged up on, then you must act swiftly and appropriately. If five kids surround you, then you are going to activate your lasers but you are not going to taser them. You will temporarily blind them with the bright light it emits, and then walk away."

"This is so cool!" Kate said. looking at her wrist, the tattoo was the size of a quarter with the gold initials of HH overlaid on it.

"In addition, it looks like an ordinary tattoo, but it's far from it. This is your panic button if you get into trouble beyond your capabilities. Tap once, and it will alert the team. We will try to extricate you from your situation. Tap twice and it's an energy source that can give you or another cyborg a jolt of thermal energy. The tattoo could also de-energize a magnetic field if you were caught in one. But it's tricky to make it work in a magnetic field. And tap three times and hold, and you can morph into whatever you want, like me turning into a helicopter or motorcycle."

"Wow! How cool is this?" Kate said. Kate closed her eyes, tapped three times, held it down and morphed into Carlita.

"Jeez, Kate, you look just like her," Kyle said. "And rocket launchers?" he asked.

"Yes, you get the update like Carlita."

"So brilliant. Mom and Dad are going to freak!" Kate said.

"Maybe that is something better off not said for a while, you think?" Harry said. "Remember, we prefer to save lives rather than to take them."

"Do we have hand rotors?" Kate asked.

"Yes, but like I told Kyle, easy does it. I need to train you," Harry said.

Kyle cracked his knuckles, his hand rotors appeared and he lifted off his bed.

"Easy, Kyle. Not so fast," Harry said.

Kate cracked her knuckles and her hand rotors appeared and she lifted off her bed.

"Okay, Kate, easy does it. That's enough for now," Harry said.

Harry stood up, "You both died out there. Still think you're cut out to be superheroes?"

Without hesitation, Kate nodded. "Heck, yeah! What other choice do we have now? Bring it on! We need to eliminate Will because he killed us and Carlita."

"Not so fast. Easier said than done. Cyborgs are hard to kill," Harry said. "It will take a virus—not just any virus but a computer virus that infects his motherboard, short-circuits it and drains him of power. Or we could generate a magnetic field to kill him, but we will have to bait him with either of you to get him to fly into it. But he could drag you into it and you would die too," Harry said. "Too risky."

"Let's use Kate as bait; I don't want to die!" Kyle said.

"Very funny, Kyle, but you will be the bait because I'm smarter and better-looking than you!" Kate said.

"Okay, stop already. We all have motherboards that power us and are incredibly hard to neutralize. We have to be careful since the virus we create cannot escape the lab. It could easily kill us if we get infected," Harry said.

"Won't our tattoos eliminate a virus or magnetic field?" Kyle said.

"To a certain extent, but they're not perfect. I'm sure you have had your computers infected in the past. Virus protection is not one-hundred percent effective. It can be

really hard to get rid of the virus, and can even destroy your computer. In the meantime, change back into your
  clothes. One more thing. You are vulnerable to death since your cyborg brains are not fully uploaded yet. Sorry to lay that on you. Just be careful if you encounter Will until tomorrow, as the upload won't be completed until then. Let's pop over to Recon Airfield and visit some old friends that are superheroes in their own right. The Badass Bros.

Badass Bros

My winds of peace are the headwind in the face of bullies!

"Okay," Harry said, "the next chapter in our super-hero bootcamp training is a visit to the Badass Bros; Windmaker and Striker. These guys are pretty bad dudes. Let's take a spin over to Recon Airfield and see if we can find them. That is, if you are feeling yourselves?"

"I feel a little freaky, maybe like a monster out of a sci-fi movie although I feel way smarter and stronger than any boy that might want to challenge me," Kate said.

"I feel like a new and improved kid. I don't feel ten but much older, like you Harry," Kyle said. "I was always good at math but now I feel like I can solve any math formula and like my new confidence too."

"Great! But don't be a show-off to the kids at school, teachers and your parents as they will become suspicious of you."

Kate and Kyle climbed into Turbo and flew to the landing spot within a few minutes.

"What is this place?" Kate asked, her eyes wide. "There must be hundreds of choppers of all sizes and colors out here. Is the time machine here too?"

"Inquiring minds just never cease, do they, Kate?" Harry said. "I promise I'll show you the time machine one day, just not today."

The twins' faces lit up; Harry quickly changed the subject. He spotted Windmaker with a few other warriors and waved for him to come over. "Let me introduce you to Windmaker, the great warrior. Kids, please don't say anything to agitate him."

Windmaker ran up in a cloud of dust, circling everyone a couple of times and gazing into the twins' eyes. He stopped and greeted Harry with a traditional bear hug. They looked at each other with big smiles, as if they were brothers who hadn't seen each other in a long time.

"Hello, Windmaker. I'd like you to meet Kyle and Kate."

The kids heard the faint sound of drums beating in the distance. They suddenly looked alert and scared. Kate whispered to Kyle, "He looks more like Running Butt Cheeks than a Windmaker!" She laughed in Kyle's ear. Kyle chuckled nervously too.

"Funny one, kid! But you're right, that is a more tradi-tional name," Windmaker said.

The mighty warrior was dressed in traditional loincloth, and his long black hair straddled his shoulders. His face was covered in red and black war paint, and he carried a bow and arrows on his right shoulder. He was a giant of a man—taller and older than Harry—and was made of pure muscle. He squeezed his right bicep, which was decorated with a tattoo of a cobra, representing strength and death. Windmaker turned to the twins and knelt on one leg so he was at eye level with them. The twins were nervous and trembled a little.

"*Greetings,* pale faces," he bellowed to the twins. "I am the mighty Windmaker, but my winds of peace blow more steadily now than the winds of war. My people became great warriors many moons ago, but our winds of war are now a warm breeze of the past."

"Wow, Windmaker," Kyle said, "you're a pretty badass dude, aren't you?"

Windmaker nodded. "Yes, son, but it's best to make peace and keep the peace."

"What's that drumming sound in the distance?" Kate asked.

"Unfortunately my people are preparing to rise against the bullies of the world that want to hurt our country. As you might know, the Apache helicopter was designed after me—a mighty warrior—to protect our lands and our people."

The twins' mouths hang open. They listened closely as Windmaker continued.

"Let me demonstrate how my arrows have been replaced with biomass missiles as I morph into the android chopper.

"Did you say biomass missiles?" Kyle asked.

"Yes, son. They're as nasty as it gets and you don't want to be anywhere near it when they go off!"

Windmaker raised his left arm straight up with a clenched fist. He let out a warrior yell that scared the twins. They stood frozen, their arms limp and jaws open. Windmaker slowly transformed into the mighty chopper. His left arm gyrated, morphing into a rotor as he lowered the bag of arrows on his right arm. His body transformed into hardened aluminum as the warrior yell faded into a whisper. The Windmaker's head then morphed into the cockpit, with each arm now an arsenal of pumpkin missiles. The smell of pumpkin biomass fuel permeated the stinky humid air.

"Wow," Kyle said. "That's so amazing, Windmaker. Maybe we can go for a ride and shoot some of your new arrows?"

"Perhaps a little later. First you must meet my brother, Striker, named after the cobra snake," Windmaker replied. "As you may know, the cobra snake has a deadly bite. Striker is sleek and stealthy, which enables him to sneak up on people, just like I do. He can strike without you even knowing what hit you, but like me he would rather keep the peace. Would you like to meet Striker?"

"Um…sure, Windmaker," Kate said, quivering a little.

"Striker, come on out," Windmaker called.

The kids turned their heads and saw many snakes coiled in the shade underneath several choppers. Striker slithered out from underneath one of the choppers, where he had been napping. He had a ten-foot-long, cold, tan, scaly body. He raised his head to the twins' height. They were looking at each other eye to eye and nose to nose when Striker opened his mouth as if he were going to swallow them. His pointy white fangs looked menacing as his red-forked tongue quickly slid in and out of his mouth, touching the twins' noses as if he were sizing them up as prey.

"Yuck," Kate said. "I don't like the feel of his sandpapery tongue touching my nose, or his camel breath."

"Sorry, kid," Striker said.

Harry laughed. "Striker appears to be gentle, doesn't he? He's a real charmer, but don't be fooled. You can pet him, but be careful." He gently stroked the back of Striker's head. "Snakes come in all sizes and colors. But there's only one cobra."

Striker swayed slightly. "Back at home in India, my venom is used to save lives, but let me charm you with my ability to become the new Striker chopper. Harry will grab my tail, swing me around and around over his head, and then let me fly. As I fly through the air, I'll morph into the chopper."

Harry bent down, grabbed Striker by the tail, and swung him overhead, until he let go on the fifth whirl.

As Striker soared skyward, he shed his skin from head to tail. Each fold of skin that peeled back revealed a new skin of hardened aluminum.

His forked tongue became a flame thrower under the nose of the chopper, which could shoot a hot stream of flames at bullies and cook them in seconds. His head transformed into the cockpit while Striker's old snake skin was grabbed by a wet breeze. It flew through the air until it slowly disappeared over the horizon.

"Wow! That's crazy. Let's go fly," Kate said. "Can we, Windmaker?"

"No way, kid," Windmaker replied.

"Come on, Striker," Kyle said. "Make us proud."

"Well, Windmaker," Striker said, "we do need to get some air time in while we wait for our orders."

Before they could decide, the twins had already made up their minds.

"I want to fly with Windmaker and fly upside down and do cool tricks with the chopper like Prince Harry."

"I'm heading for Striker!" Kyle exclaimed.

Kate climbed into Windmaker, and Kyle climbed into Striker.

"Well, kids," Striker said, "now that you're warriors, you'll need to put on your warrior armor."

The twins slipped on helmets that were in the seat beside them. They each let out an ear-piercing warrior yell.

Kate shouted, "Woh-who-ey! Who-ey! Who-ey!"

Kyle shouted, "Woh-who-ey! Who-ey! Who-ey!"

They were both grinning wildly when Windmaker said, "Alright, kids. Enough already. These choppers fly a little differently from the ones Harry has shown you, but I'm sure you'll pick it up quickly."

"Kyle," Striker said, "you should have no problem since you're flying the Cobra, which has enhanced controls."

"Looks like my game controller at home," Kyle said with a grin.

Striker laughed. "You've been training to be a pilot all these years, and you didn't even know it."

The twins fired up the choppers, and the feeling of empowerment took over.

They lifted off and were about a thousand feet off the ground when Kyle radioed Kate.

"Are you having fun, Kate?"

"Yeah, this is awesome," she said. "Check it out, Kyle. We're flying upside down in a roll. I'm ready for a mission! We need to save the world from trouble-makers."

"Great idea," Kyle said. "Let's save the world!"

"Hold that thought, kids," Windmaker said. "Sorry. We aren't saving the world today. However, we do have an endless war within our borders that requires attention at the moment. Are you interested?"

The children's faces lit up.

"You bet, but it better not be boring!" Kyle said.

"Okay," Windmaker replied. "You can test out the new laser that we have been working on and the missiles on the small town of Sundown, nestled in the desert along the California border with Mexico. We got a tip that this town used to be a pumpkin biomass treatment plant that shut down a few years ago. Biomass is an organic GMO (also known as *genetically modified organism)* that has many uses, such as fuel. Sundown became a ghost town until Will and his bullies happened upon it. They use the left-over pumpkin seeds and pulp and combine them to make illegal genetically altered pumpkins. When the pumpkin seeds are mixed with organic biofuel, it becomes a syner-gistic fuel through a neutralizing process of methane gas and then becomes fuel for Will's aircraft. This orange biomass energy enables some helicopters and planes to fly at the speed of light. But this is counterfeit biofuel and it only runs in their aircraft which gives them an edge over us. Although we have our own lethal biofuel, it's no match for the counterfeit. That's only the half of it. If it's sold on the black market to bullies around the world, it'll jeopardize the safety of our country. One gallon of pumpkin biofuel can fetch a million dollars on the black market."

"I would have never known what biomass is until I got my cyborg brain. I just did a quick internet search in my minds' eye, and found so many uses for it. Who would have known there are so many uses for biomass, from fuel to missiles?" Kyle said.

"Androids know, as the seeds are a biomass energy in themselves." said Windmaker.

"So you're an android too?" Kyle said.

"Yup, how did you guess?"

"You changing into a helicopter did it!" Kyle said.

"Holy cow," Kate said. "Does this have anything to do with Harry's time machine?"

"Sorta, as it does run on biofuel," Striker said. "The world's fuel reserves have dwindled to the point where competition for new kinds of fuel is higher than ever. That's why Windmaker and I are on the lookout for spies. Remember Otis was on a scouting mission for new places to grow? Although these fields near the town of Sundown are full of mature pumpkins, we can't use them for our aircraft because they are counterfeit. But we still have a surprise for bullies. We're going to help them harvest the pumpkins, but not quite like they planned. Have you ever heard the term *shock and awe*?"

"We have now because I just watched a clip of you both from the internet," Kyle said.

"Ha! I was miles ahead of you, Kyle. I didn't need to watch a silly video as the term Shock and Awe is assimilated on the net with the Badass Bros and I just opened it up. Get with the program, Kyle!" said Kate.

"Well, we are the Badass Bros. that deliver the shock and awe also known as overwhelming power!" Windmaker added, "And when Striker and I finish with a mission, everything usually goes up in smoke."

"We know already!" Kate said.

"Don't be a smartypants, Kate," Kyle said.

"Hey, Windmaker," Striker said. "We're about five miles from Sundown. How about you and Kate take out the pumpkin crop?"

"Ten-four, buddy," Windmaker said. "Okay, Kate. It's harvest time. Bank the chopper and come in from the north. That's right: left pedal, and stick to the left."

"Look how dry and brown the desert is, Windmaker," Kate said. "And then you see a forest of green and orange sparkling in the sunshine. Those pumpkins look as big as cars!"

"Yes, Kate," Windmaker said. "That's what can happen when you tinker with Mother Nature. There are acres of pumpkins worth millions of dollars that we're going to incinerate within minutes. We'll swoop in low, mow down the fields with the laser, finish with a couple of missile strikes, and set the whole thing ablaze. Then we'll back off, watch the crop go up in smoke, and see if Striker needs any help. Kate, the yellow button for the new laser is on the stick. The flying might get tricky for you. Just remember your ABCs. Let's drop down over this big crop so you can incinerate it with the laser.

"What's a laser?" Kate asked.

"You should know this if your cyborg app is updated correctly. But if not, I will address this. It's made of heated sun rays that destroys anything in its path," Windmaker said. "Go ahead and ease the collective down and start firing some missiles with the orange button on the stick."

KABOOM! Large explosions appeared in the distance. The sound of the missiles intensified as they struck the fields.

"So these missiles are packed full of methane gas from the sludge?" Kate asked.

"Yes, they are," Windmaker said.

"What a blast this is," Kate said.

Pieces of pumpkins as large as cows went flying through the air and splattered the windshield.

Meanwhile, Striker and Kyle were setting their sights on the processing plant.

"Whoa.—this place looks pretty deserted. Maybe they're gone," Kyle said.

"It's nap time in the shade, so let's make this quick. We'll swoop low and fire about ten pumpkin sludge missiles," Striker said.

"Ten-four, Striker," Kyle replied. "The processing plant is in my sights."

"Yes, indeed," Striker said. "Good eye, Kyle. Give the red button on the stick a big squeeze, and then sit back and smoke them."

The missiles flew off in a frenzy of trailing smoke. An explosion echoed in the near distance as the building was blown to pieces. As they flew over the smoldering processing plant, they saw pumpkin sludge scattered amongst bodies in the ruins of the demolished building.

"I see what you mean," Kyle said. "Just gotta love the shock and awe as everything goes up in smoke."

Windmaker shouted to Kate, "Great job! That's a wrap. Based on how much smoke is in the air, I think we accomplished our mission. This is reminiscent of days gone by when my people communicated with smoke signals."

"What are these smoke signals telling you, Windmaker?" Kate asked.

"They're telling me that my awesome bro, Striker, has stunk the place up, and it's time to head back to base."

"You know we are cyborgs and can be pretty tough like you," Kate said.

"So I heard," Windmaker said. "Has Harry taught you how to fight yet?"

"Not really," Kate said. "We came pre-programmed as ninja fighters, though."

"Should we go back and let you fight the stragglers that didn't die?" Windmaker asked. "You do know you have superhuman strength, so most humans are really no match for you."

"You're with me, so game on," Kate said. "Call Striker so my brother can be part of the ground and pound."

Windmaker radioed Striker to return and let Kyle do some ground and pound. They both landed and Kate and Kyle exited the choppers. Then the choppers morphed into the Indian and the snake. The twins immediately started chasing people as Kate jumped on the back of a man and knocked him to the ground. He jumped up and tried to fight her, but she was too quick. She swung around backward, kicked him in the face and knocked him out.

"Oh my god, this is so fun. I feel like a Ninja Warrior!" Kate said.

"Yeah, not just a warrior but a badass warrior!" Windmaker said as he grabbed two burly men and slammed them into each other. Striker was coiled around another man, squeezing the life out of him while biting his neck. Meanwhile, Kyle was battling three men with shaved heads with his new warrior skills. The three men had him surrounded and were closing in on him. But Kyle spun super fast, delivering kicks and punches where all the men were knocked out cold, if not dead.

Then two more guys came running towards Kyle and he zapped them with an orange bolt of energy. They cried out and collapsed.

"Nice one," Kate said. "They smell well done!"

"You guys had your fun?" Striker asked.

"Oh my god, this is incredible. No more being bullied at school," Kyle said.

"Okay, let's pick up our drum and beat it back to base," Windmaker said.

"Not so fast!" A voice called out from the wrecked building. Will and his girlfriend walked out with arms folded. "You ready to get your fight on, punks? You ruined my base of operations!" Additional men and kids lined up behind him.

Kate and Kyle looked at each other and felt initimidated like at the park when they got black eyes. Will looked menacing without half his human face. His red eye glowed like a laser encased in his metal eye socket.

"Okay, sis. They are bigger than us but we can take them, right?"

"Yeah, we owe you some black eyes, losers!" Kate yelled.

"Maybe we should call Harry," Kyle said. "Or tap our tattoo to get extricated?" Kyle tapped on his tattoo.

"Nothing is happening! The cyborg app must not be uploaded yet," he said to Kate and showed Will his tattoo by holding up his arm.

Will laughed and said, "Time to die again, punk!"

Kate tried to call Harry and got a network error message that said: *need to connect to wifi.*

"Geez, Kyle, this cyborg app isn't all that it's cracked up to be."

"Go ahead and run, you big babies," Will's girlfriend, Karen, said.

"I know, it's still uploading. This one is on us, Kate. Do or die. Remember what Harry said. Pretend we are at school and picture the playground bullies that pick on us all the time," Kyle said.

Kate visualized Roy, a tall skinny boy as tall as Will, and a girl, Becky, with dirty black knotty hair. Becky often pulled Kate's hair, spat at her and called her names. "Done! Let's get them!" Kate said.

"You got this, kids!" Windmaker yelled out while grappling with a man.

"Ha! You think your new cyborg bodies are going to save you from the destruction that awaits!" Will said."

"He has a point, Kyle," Kate said.

"I know. We are vulnerable to death since we aren't fully uploaded cyborgs yet. But we aren't going to get bullied again without a fight."

The twins each took a large gulp of air, burped loudly and fired their hand lasers at Will and Karen. Kate hit the girl in the stomach, and Kyle hit Will in the face. Kate and Kyle raced up to them while they were stunned and ninja-kicked them in the face and stomach. They dropped to the ground as Kate and Kyle punched and kicked them. But Will and his girlfriend bounced up and beat down Kate and Kyle. They were on the ground, and Kyle fired his rocket launcher into the belly of Will which sent him flying into a smoking building. Kate fired her rocket launcher in his girlfriend's face, and she flew fifty yards. She landed on top of Will with half her face singed off. They were now both half-faced with one beady red eye.

"Hey, losers, how do y'all like our new upgrades since we last met in the park!"

Windmaker and Striker got charged by a group of men and dogpiled. Windmaker threw them off and grabbed Striker by the tail, and began whipping several of the men. They were all cyborgs and it barely fazed them. Two men came up behind Windmaker, grabbed his large arms, twisted him to the ground, and stepped on his head, trying to crush it. He broke loose, grabbed one and power-slammed him head-first into the ground. Then Windmaker grabbed the other. He lifted him above his shoulders and power-bombed him to the dirt. He ran over to a destroyed truck that was smoldering and climbed on top of the cab. He stretched out his arms and did a flying drop, nailing both men in the head with a clothesline and knocking them out. More men surrounded him, and he ran over to a group of rocks. He picked up a rock, the size of a boulder, raised it over his head with both arms and released it with a mighty force, smashing them with it. Striker slithered over to finish them off with rapid bites and slapped their faces with his tail.

"Never say die, as we will be back to fight another day, losers!" Will and his girlfriend flew off.

"Nice job, kids, Harry would be proud," Windmaker said.

"Yeah, you did a nice smackdown on those bullies," Kate said.

"I was a pro wrestler in my previous life, which really helps me as an undefeated cyborg," Windmaker said. "You should come watch me and Jackaroo on Saturday nights for Cyborg Smackdown. We are a tag team and this isn't fake wrestling. We take Smackdown to the extreme and shred."

"Sounds like fun. Ya think, Kyle?" Kate said.

"You bet and maybe we can get in the ring and work on our Smackdown skills."

"You were, right Kyle, with imagining beating up the bullies at school!" Kate said.

"That was fun alright," Kyle said. "How do you feel, Kate? That was some pretty hard-core fighting you did with the rocket launchers."

"I feel good. These cyborg bodies are to die for! We both took a beating and gave one back," Kate said.

Windmaker and Striker morphed into the choppers and The twins climbed back in and took off. They soon landed back at Recon Airfield, where Harry greeted them.

"Holy cow, way to go, kids! You performed better than I thought you would."

"Yeah, we got to fight in hand-to-hand combat and kicked butt!" Kate said.

"And the Badass Bros are badass!" Kyle said. "They both have incredible striking ability. And *wow*, what an awesome adventure that was! I just might want to come back and be a fighter pilot."

"They're both lean, mean, fighting machines, Harry!" Kyle said. "Wooo! We got to go on a mission!"

"Fantastic! And great job on your successful mission against Will and crazy Karen," Harry said, patting Kyle's head. "You've now entered the world of superheroes. Sam the Man would be proud."

"Let us know if we can help you again, Windmaker," Kate said.

"Sure, kid. We'll be giving you a call soon." Windmaker and Striker flew off. "We just might do that," Windmaker told Striker, "They did better than expected."

Kyle pointed toward a distant group of Black Hawk helicopters flying in formation.

Harry glanced at his watch and back at the kids. "We have one more team member to visit while we are here. Let me see if one of those is Sergeant Major. I think that's her carrying the truck." He called on his radio, "Hey, Sergeant Major, it's Harry. Do you have time to come down for a chat?"

Sergeant Major acknowledged him. "Harry? Really? I'll be right down."

She circled the airfield a few times, lowered the Humvee into position on the tarmac, and landed. The sun reflected off her sleek black body. Sergeant Major was a hardened war veteran who had been on numerous tours of duty around the world.

"Hey, good-looking," she said. "I see you have some kids with you. You know this area is restricted, Harry."

"What's the big deal, Sergeant Major?" Kate snickered. "We're just a couple of ten-year-olds. What harm can we do?" She poked Kyle and giggled.

"It's okay," Harry said. "They're the Copter Kids in training to be superheroes. They just became cyborgs."

"I see," Sergeant Major said. "You're tough kids now. Okay, let's get started. I need to deliver this Humvee. Do you guys want to come?"

"Can I ask, what do you do?" Kyle said.

"Well, young man, I am in charge of the pumpkin biomass missile program. It takes a lot a of sludge to make these missiles explode like they're supposed to and to make the world safe from the crazy bullies. Does that make sense?"

"Yes, but can we get a ride on your back before you make the delivery?" Kate asked.

"Excuse me, but this isn't a carnival!" Sergeant Major quipped. "Don't you have hand rotors now?"

"Yes, but we aren't trained yet."

"It's okay. The team has been giving them short rides along the way," Harry said.

"Okay, but let's make this quick. We have a lot of preparation to do." Sergeant Major morphed from a chopper into an enormous black hawk and the twins climbed on her back for a short flight over the airfield.

"This is better than any carnival ride, Sergeant Major!" Kyle shouted.

"Kate, look closely for the time machine as we swoop over the other choppers." Kyle said.

"Okay, but there are so many choppers, and I don't think I'd know it if I did see it," Kate said.

"Me either," said Kyle. "Man, I'm blown away by this flight over this place. We sure are lucky to get this tour."

"Yeah, it's hard to put into words. There are so many machines that I've never seen before."

"What's up with the underpants as a wind sock?" Kyle asked.

"That's our good friend Jackaroo. He thought it was funny to swap out all the wind socks with his underpants so we never forget about him. He can be so goofy, but that's why we love him," Sergeant Major said.

"So funny," Kate said.

Sergeant Major descended and touched down on the tarmac.

"Thanks so much!" Kate said as she and Kyle climbed off.

On the tarmac, Sergeant Major morphed back into the Black Hawk chopper, and then Harry attached cables to the Humvee so she could transport it. Harry and the twins climbed inside the helicopter and were airborne within minutes. The twins sat quietly.

"This looks a lot different from the other choppers we've seen today," Kate said, as she examined all the knobs, buttons, and gauges. "It looks much more complicated."

"Oh, yes," Sergeant Major bragged. "We Black Hawks are more sophisticated than our predecessors. Did you know I replaced that old rust bucket of bolts, Helicopter Huey?"

"Yeah, we heard about that," Kate said. "Did you ever take a bullet like Huey did?"

Sergeant Major laughed. "Oh, he must've bent your ear with one of his war stories, bless his heart. Yes, as a matter of fact. I was transporting a young man that was wounded. There's no greater honor than helping a soldier. During that flight, some hostiles shot a rocket-propelled grenade and blew a hole as big as your head in my right side. Funny thing, the missile didn't explode; it just went right through my left side and out the right. Lucky thing, it wasn't one of our missiles or I would have been a goner for sure. Talk about making your rotor spin! I didn't stop spinning until I crashed into a sand dune."

"Wow, another wounded warrior. Did the Badass Bros, Windmaker and Striker come to your rescue?" Kyle asked.

"Oh, yes. They were pretty upset when they heard I had gone down, especially helping injured soldiers," Sergeant Major said. "They were smoking mad and came real quick. They hooked a cable to me and brought me to a safe zone. Then they went back to deliver their shock and awe and really stunk the place up with their biomass missiles. Boy, talk about a couple of studs strutting their shiny aluminum. I sure love a chopper in uniform." Sergeant Major blushed. "I did get a Purple Heart, though, and I wear it proudly on my visor. Hey, look at the scars, under my left and right windows."

The kids looked at the patched holes inside the cockpit and rubbed their hands over them, feeling the rivets with their fingertips.

"Wow, that's awesome you survived that near-death experience," Kyle said.

"And you can lift a truck. You're like those muscle men we met earlier," Kate said.

"Oh, yes, but I'm an android like the rest of the team. You met the muscle men? Once they get juiced, there's no stopping them."

"Where are you taking the truck, Sergeant Major?" Harry asked.

"I'm transporting it to the motor pool so the boys can install the new laser. We'll be able to strike down trouble-maker aircraft with a hot beam of light. And as you may already know, we're preparing for a mission," she said.

"Windmaker and Striker are awaiting their orders. I wouldn't be surprised if they activated you, Harry. It sounds pretty big."

They dropped off the truck at the motor pool at the far end of Recon Airfield, where all the vehicles were serviced. Then they flew back to where they had started.

"Are you going to save the world or some country, Sergeant Major?" Kyle asked as they landed.

"Sorry, son," she said. "We're off to rampage! That's all I know."

"We understand. You're on a mission," Kyle said.

"Thanks, Sergeant Major," Kate added. "You're one of the coolest birds we've met today, and you make it all look so easy."

"Just another bird in our group of androids," Sergeant Major said. "Harry, will you contact Calypso, her special team and Will and put them on alert?"

"Uh, didn't you hear, Will went rogue and attacked Calypso, knocking Kate into the ocean, while making a rescue. Kyle went in after her and they both drowned. They were rebuilt into cyborgs," Harry said.

"What! You mean Will? He was like a little brother to you. And now, Will is the rogue who killed these beautiful children?" Sergeant Major said. "No way!"

"Yes way, and the twins just did battle with him and his girlfriend!" Harry said. "And he's public enemy number one!"

"Remind me, how old is this punk and what does he look like now?"

"He's about thirteen, five feet ten, brown hair, purple baseball cap, turned backward, Levis and purple tennis shoes. He has a white T-shirt that has AS on it," Harry said.

"And what does AS stand for?"

"Adults suck!" Harry said.

"That sounds like a typical rebel teenager!" she said.

"Yes, but he is anything but typical and he has to be neutralized!" Harry said. "He might try to kill us all."

"Good luck with that, Harry. He is one of yours that you mentored, which will be difficult," Sergeant Major said.

"I know. And I think the rest of the team is already on alert," Harry said.

"Okay, it's time to go, kids."

"We'll be seeing you, Sergeant Major," Harry said.

"Nice seeing you again, Harry," she said. "Take care, and keep an eye on Kate and Kyle."

Sergeant Major's rotor disappeared into her body. The cockpit transformed back into her head and into big black eyes as the helicopter body morphed into a black hawk bird.

Her long black wings were fully extended. She thrust them upward and shook off a couple of large tail feathers, which floated down to the tarmac. Kate thought she could pick one up, but it was six feet long and too big to carry. Sergeant Major circled around the airfield a couple of times and then zoomed off into the big blue sky.

"Hey, Harry." Kyle pointed up. "What's that chopper way up in the sky? It's been following us. It doesn't look like a normal chopper."

"That's just Chantal," Harry said. "She's working surveillance."

"Really? That's Chantal?" Kate asked. "So Chantal can morph too?"

Splat! Bird poop landed on Kyle's hat.

"What the...!" Kyle said, as Kate and Harry laughed.

"Consider that a drone strike! That's Chantal just letting you know she reads you loud and clear." Harry said. "Oh, yeah, can she morph! I know she's listening to our conversation as we speak; she's the stealthy drone. She soars like no other, but I'll let her fill you in." As Harry said this, Chantal swooped down and landed.

"No windshield?" Kyle asked.

Then Chantal started to shake. Her color changed from sandstone to blue-green as feathers popped out of the fuselage. The rotor dropped into wings, and the tail rotor changed into a fluffy feathered tail. The nose of the chopper shrank into Chantal's beak as she began to speak. Chantal was now a giant android hummingbird.

"Sorry for the poop strike on your hat, Kyle and yes, kids, I've been watching you on your journey. Now that you're in our world of superheroes, it's my job to keep an eye on you. Don't you just love surprises?"

"You bet, Chantal," Kate said.

"I've been watching and listening to you guys from thirty thousand feet away. I'm a stealthy bird and I've got the newest, most exciting technology—it'll blow your mind. I can even become invisible. Watch as I activate my invisible shield and become the stealthiest of the stealthy."

All of a sudden, Chantal vanished into thin air.

"What?" Kyle said. "Where did you go? How did you do that? It's magic?"

"It's android magic," Chantal said. "My outer skin is made of electromagnetic material that reflects light when I activate it." Just recently the technology became available for us androids," she explained as she became visible again. "As technology develops, we'll be able to hide everything, even you and me."

"Gotta run, kids. A radio message just came in. And I got word about a pending drone strike. I have to go pick up biomass missiles."

"Can we have a ride on your back before you leave?" Kate asked.

"Why not?" Chantal said. "But just a short one."

The twins hopped on behind her neck, and she became invisible again. She zoomed up five hundred feet and flew down to Harry. Then she zoomed over his head, blowing off his hat.

Harry yelled, "Thanks a lot!" He shook his fist. The twins laughed.

Finally, she morphed into the drone chopper and became visible again, setting down to let the kids out.

"See you later, kids!" Chantal called out as she took off.

Kate and Kyle waved good-bye to her.

Kyle looked at Kate. "Wow! Wasn't that the coolest ride? It was like flying on a magic carpet!"

"Oh, yeah, totally the coolest thing ever!" Kate said. "Hey, Kyle, you were supposed to ask Chantal about the time machine."

He shrugged. "I know, but I didn't feel comfortable doing that after Sergeant Major was suspicious about us. Anyway, maybe the time machine is invisible, and we'll never find it."

"We should be moving on," Harry said.

The twins wiped their faces and looked at one another, letting out a sigh of relief.

BRUTUS

I eat bullies!

B rutus swooped down, landed not far from Harry and the twins, and walked over to them.

"Hey, Brutus," Harry said. "What brings you around?"

"My ears picked up chatter in your area, and I wasn't sure what I heard."

"You heard us yapping. As you know, these children are my new cyborg protégés." Harry said. "And they didn't make it past Captain Calypso before Will killed them."

"Looks like you owe me one, Harry. Nobody thought they would make it this far," Brutus said.

"Yup, I owe you!" Harry said. "I was completely blindsided. I thought we'd get past you, if not finish completely."

"What are you guys talking about? Were you betting on our lives? Is this some kind of superhero game?" Kyle asked.

"Uh, yeah, sorta," Harry said.

"We scored you on each stage of your bootcamp and I got to eat the one with the lowest score," Brutus joked.

"Yeah, right. Real funny. So, how many kids have died going through this bootcamp game of yours?" Kate said.

Harry looked at Brutus and said, "Do you remember?"

"No, but I know I ate a lot of them," Brutus said.

"I thought you said you only ate bullies?" Kyle asked.

"Yes, you are right—bullies and spies that pretend not to be bullies. I'm sure you know kids like that at your school. When we catch them, they can never leave, so I eat them. My nickname is *The—Enforcer.*"

Brutus gave a reassuring smile. "However, there are more that I didn't eat. And we have teams all over the world combating bullies. It won't be long until they are called upon to take down Will and his gang of bullies," Harry said.

"Oh my god, Brutus, you are so awesome. We really need you at our school, like I said earlier."

"No, I think you have it under control, now that you are cyborgs. No bully can hurt you."

"Thanks to Kate for not clipping in, which got us both killed," Kyle said.

"But look on the bright side, Kyle. We are now cyborgs and have hand rotors and can never die, and no one can hurt us," Kate exclaimed.

"My bad," Kyle said.

Brutus bent down and offered his claws to shake. Kate shook his left claw, while Kyle shook his right claw. "Congratulations, you made it! No hard feelings?"

"Sure, Brutus. Can we go for a ride on your back?" Kate asked.

"You sure know how to work it, don't you, Kate?" Harry joked.

"Well, you owe us after that shenanigan!" Kate said. "Maybe it was your plan all along to get us killed?"

"Kate, you're letting your human emotions get to you. I gave you both plenty of opportunities to quit, and you said no," Harry agreed.

"You're right," Kate said.

"What do you mean, she knows how to work it?" Brutus asked.

"She's gotten everyone on the team to give both of them a ride." Harry laughed.

Brutus nudged Harry and then scratched his chin with the tip of his wing. "How's Captain Calypso anyway? It's been ages since we last flew together. She'd just gotten out of the Naval Warfare asset program the last time we spoke. She is a special asset and a mighty fine chopper."

"She's the coolest dolphin ever!" Kyle said.

"And *wow*, can she fly!" Kate said.

"And can Captain Calypso fly upside down?" Brutus asked. "Because I sure can!"

Kate and Kyle looked at each other with anticipation.

"Let's take a quick ride, and I'll show my outrageous abilities," Brutus said.

"Just don't eat us," Kate said. She and Kyle laughed hysterically.

"I could swallow you whole!" Brutus laughed, opened his big brown leathery jaws as wide as he could and wiggled his pinkish tongue. The twins looked nervous until Kate yelled down his mouth, "Hello, is anyone down there?"

"Yes, I need help. Stretch your arm down and pull me out!" Brutus said in a little boy's voice and played along and joked with the twins. He closed his jaws, and gave them a wink and a smile.

"So, Sergeant Major told us biomass missiles are made from pumpkin pulp," Kate said.

"That is correct and they're quite deadly!"

"Thanks for the heads-up Brutus." Kate poked Kyle.

Kate climbed on behind the horn on Brutus's head, and Kyle got on behind her.

Kyle whispered in Kate's ear, "Remember when we would ride on Grandpa's back?"

Kate gave a nod. "Yeah, those were the best days."

"Are you guys holding on tight?" Brutus asked. "Let me know if you get scared."

With a couple of powerful wing thrusts, they lifted off, and the kids could feel the turbulent air pass over their bodies. As they soared through the blue sky to one thousand feet, Kyle yelled, "Hey, Kate, look at Harry down there. He looks like a kid from up here."

Brutus rotated his head back toward the children, almost pulling them off.

"You're right. Shall we pay him a visit?"

The twins screamed with joy as Brutus rolled over and corkscrewed toward the ground.

"This is better than an amusement park ride!" Kate yelled.

"You got that right, sis. Even more fun than Machismo and Calypso!" Kyle said, as they flipped upright again.

"Time for some real fun," Brutus said. "Watch as I begin my androidmation." His fingers transformed into giant propellers, and his wings morphed into the wings of an airplane. They were flying really fast when the twins' hats flew off and floated to the ground.

Kyle nudged Kate. "Looks like it's going to be a bad hair day for you."

She shrugged and said to Brutus, "Too much wind. I don't think we can hang on much longer."

Then both kids somersaulted backward and fell off two hundred feet above the ground.

Kate screamed, piercing Kyle's eardrum and Kyle yelled, "Engage your hand rotors!"

Kate did so by cracking her knuckles. "Nice to be flying, Kyle," Kate said.

"Yeah, this is so cool. No more carnival rides because we have our own hand rotors," Kyle said.

Brutus was half chopper and half pterodactyl as his tan body transformed into the helicopter's fuselage. He landed.

"These hand rotors rock," Kate said.

"So fun," Kyle added.

"You got the hang of it pretty quick," Brutus said. "Let's pick up Harry and take a spin out to the ocean and back."

"Sounds like a plan," Kate said. The twins entered the aircraft and took their seats in the cockpit. Kate studied the control panel as Brutus lifted off. The cockpit was larger and more complicated than the others.

"Don't touch anything, Kate!" Kyle exclaimed.

She turned to Kyle and smiled. "I won't." The rotors tilted up, and they made their approach to land like a helicopter.

When they set down, Brutus said, "Open the back door for Harry, Kyle. Pull the orange lever that says exit."

"Okay," Kyle said.

"Duh," Kate muttered.

Harry climbed in, took a seat, and handed the twins' hats back to them.

"Thanks, Harry," Kate and Kyle said in unison.

"We're going to take a spin out to the ocean," Brutus said.

Harry smiled. "Sure thing."

"Oh, this is going to be another roller-coaster ride. I can just tell," Kate said and smiled anxiously.

Harry fired up the chopper and told her, "Grab the collective, and gently pull up. Kyle, take the yoke—also known as the steering wheel, and keep her steady."

"Sam the Man said he can fly four hundred miles an hour. Is he faster than you, Brutus?" Kyle asked.

"Ah, another tall tale from Sam," said Brutus. "I'm afraid the Copter Cop was pulling your leg. He'd be lucky to go two hundred miles an hour with the wind at his back."

"So tell me, Brutus," Kyle said. "What's the purpose of this mighty machine?"

"Well, Kyle, if I don't eat bullies, I transfer them to a detention camp, where the boss decides if they can be rehabilitated and turned into something useful. If not, I dispose of them. Will is always recruiting, and we try to intercept him before he turns youngsters into bullies."

Brutus lifted off like a normal helicopter, with the tilt rotors up.

"Kate, flip the black lever to lower the rotors," Harry said.

Kate did as instructed and smiled proudly. The rotors lowered to a horizontal position, like the propellers on an airplane, Brutus sped upward, soaring to an altitude of five-thousand feet. They were screaming along at three-hundred miles an hour over the ocean, when they suddenly heard a loud crunch into the side of the chopper. For no apparent reason, the tilt rotors flipped up as if Brutus were going to land.

Everyone's heads snapped backward and hit the backs of their seats. "Ow!" said Kyle, rubbing his head.

"It's Will. He is trying to take control of Brutus and crash us. He grabbed the rotors and tilted them up. He

thinks we are transporting bullies and wants to intercept them for his elite group for world domination. But we have a surprise for him. Brutus, I need you to morph back into the pterodactyl. We will try to grab Will and place him into your mouth. Maybe we can end him. Twins, get ready to engage your hand rotors. We will grab Will and hold him for the jaws of death."

"Ten-four Harry," Kyle said, "but can we do this?"

"We can sure try," Kate said.

Brutus transformed into the pterodactyl, with everyone exposed in mid-air. This caught Will off guard, and Harry grabbed Will's legs while Kate and Kyle each grabbed an arm. They struggled to stay aloft with each only having one rotor flying. Brutus flew near them with his mouth wide open. He was a scary sight to behold with his sharp white teeth and his gross-looking jaws waiting to devour

Will. Will struggled free from Kate and Kyle's grasp but Harry still held his legs as they twirled through the air. Kate punched him in the face as did Kyle which stunned him long enough for Kate and Kyle to each grab an arm. Brutus inched closer, and opened his mouth. Harry forced Will's legs in as Kate and Kyle forced the arms in and Brutus slammed his jaws shut.

"Let me outta here," Will shouted.

Brutus's eyes were bulging as he tried to keep his mouth closed. His teeth had bits and pieces of Will's clothes on them. But Brutus couldn't swallow him because Will was too big. Harry and the twins flew onto Brutus, Harry grabbing the horn and Kate and Kyle behind. Will tried to punch his way out of Brutus's mouth, managing to create a space between Brutus's teeth. Kate and Kyle could see his arm sticking out between the upper and lower beak and they screamed.

"He's going to get out, Harry!" Kate shouted.

Harry then flipped over Brutus's horn, landed on his beak, and put his hands around it, trying to prevent Will from escaping. Brutus couldn't talk because his mouth was shut, so Harry couldn't communicate but could only give commands and hope Brutus understood. Kate was holding onto the stubby horn, and Kyle was behind, getting whipped in the face by Kate's hair.

"Brutus is going to get tired and lose his grip," Harry said. Then Will punched Brutus in his upper mouth several times, trying to loosen the grip. Harry was struggling to hold on when Will pushed open Brutus's jaws and squirmed out. "See ya, losers!" he said and flew off.

"Sorry, Harry. He is a strong one," Brutus said.

"Yes, I know. There will be other chances. It's time we moved on. See you later, Brutus. Care to join me, kids?"

The twins engaged their hand rotors and flew off with Harry and landed on the ground.

"You're getting pretty good with those hand rotors," Harry said. He motioned for them to go.

"You almost had him, Harry," Kate said.

"Yes, that's the way it goes with Will. I'll get him one day. We should be going."

Kyle stepped into the pilot seat. "Mind if I fly us back, Harry?"

"Be my guest, young man."

They once again took off like a shooting star and arrived back at the heliport in no time.

Superhero Adventure Lands

Never look back on what could have been!

Kyle set the chopper down for a smooth landing, and they all exited onto the tarmac.

"Well done, Kyle. Perfect landing," Harry said, "You guys came looking to learn about helicopters, and you go home as superhero cyborgs." He checked his watch. "Consider yourselves prepared when the world needs you to take on bullies. But being a superhero has its challenges, as you found out. Again, sorry you guys died, but you are greater than you were when we met."

"We know, Harry. Wow, what a totally awesome day!" Kate exclaimed. "I've never been so scared this much in one day."

"Yeah, and you beat death," Harry said. "Well, sorta."

"How do we explain we are cyborgs to our parents?" Kate said.

"You don't. You go on as if nothing happened. Your parents might freak," Harry said.

"Yeah, they don't want us to be pilots, let alone cyborgs so what's the use of bringing it up."

"I'll bet they will be understanding over time. But you look like your past selves. Maybe just don't say a word, and become an attorney and an engineer. Those aren't bad careers," Harry said.

"That's funny, Harry. Now that we are superhero cyborgs, are you trying to make us drown in our own barf? Gag me already!" Kyle said.

Kate and Kyle fist-bumped each other, and laughed.

"Okay, suit yourselves," Harry said.

Kyle said, "Yeah, I can't wait to go back to school, show everyone our hand rotors, and knock out porky Paul, the bully!"

"And Cindy, with the knotty black hair that stinks!" Kate said.

"Not so fast, Kyle. You aren't humans anymore and there is no knocking out bullies. You will blend in and if you use force, it's a palm to the forehead. Cyborgs and humans coexist on a daily basis but we do it on the sly." Harry's watch erupted with a voice that sounded British. *"Do you read me Q? Q, do you read me?"*

"Hold on a sec, kids," Harry said. "I have to take this."

He stepped back, raised his wrist to his ear, whispered into his watch for a minute, and then returned.

"I have an important mission that needs my attention. I need to report to Recon Airfield immediately for a briefing."

"So you *are* a British spy?"

"Well...yeah, I guess you could say that. I report to both the United States and MI6, the UK's secret service."

"My inner cyborg has determined you're a sporty, suave British guy who has an air about him, whoever you are, said Kyle.

Harry looked a little sheepish. "The guys call me GQ, if you must know."

"That's so James Bond of you," Kate said, chuckling.

"What kind of mission are you going on?" Kyle asked.

"We intercepted radio chatter from Will and his gang of bullies. They seized the pumpkin biomass missiles that are being stored at MI6 headquarters in England and they have taken prisoners."

"Sounds serious, Harry," Kyle said. "Do you need our help?"

"Yes, but let me text you from the location as this might be our chance to eliminate Will. I'm sure he is baiting us again with his band of thug-borgs."

"What are thug-borgs, Harry?" Kate asked.

"They are a group of teenage cyborgs that dropped out of school because they hated authority and wanted to rule the adults. A bunch of dimwits that will never amount to anything but trouble, and they keep multiplying. Trouble is all they know, and they're a threat that needs to be eliminated. But that's the challenge," Harry said.

"Why do you keep looking at your watch?" Kate asked.

Harry laughed. "I broke it when I crashed earlier today, and I keep checking to see if the clock has started working again. It appears the day got away from me."

"Can't they be killed with a virus or the magnetic field you spoke about?" Kyle asked.

"Cyborgs can become infected with a virus and die. Although that's rare. You must run your virus scan everyday to look for potential threats. You're online 24/7, and a simple virus can sneak in and get you. It's the only way to stay clean and inoculated. If you miss a day, it's not so bad. But if you miss a week, you're opening the door for infection and possibly death," Harry said. "But your tattoos can help with that. And keep in mind, you must still know your ABCs. Surprisingly, a lot of kids don't know their ABC's. Remember when we first met, you said you knew your ABCs, and I said not the *ones that count*? Those are the ones that will carry you through life's difficulties. If you remember nothing else from this day, remember *the ABCs that count*. They truly are what separate *you* from humans."

"Okay, Harry," Kyle said. "But is there more to the bullies than you're telling us?"

"Like I said, they're bullies. They show a disrespect for authority, which is how Will became the leader he is today," Harry said.

Harry looked at the twins, "I have you both on speed dial and a team member might contact you as well."

"You're my hero!" Kate cried.

"Oh—stop, Kate."

"Tell me, Q—or GQ—are you actually Prince Harry?" Kyle asked.

"Why would you ask such a thing?"

"My intellectual cyborg brain has determined that you are, after running a test on your voice and skin. Yes, I took a skin swab from your neck when we were on your back which my sensors indicated you don't just look and sound like him but you are him!" Kyle said.

"If I were, I couldn't tell you because then my cover would be blown. Now if I were—and I'm not saying I am—it would sorta be like Batman and Bruce Wayne or Superman and Clark Kent. But I will tell you that I have a disdain for bullies as you have seen through this training."

"And after my face recognition software finished scanning millions of images through the algorithm I wrote in a matter of seconds, my sophisticated cyborg brain has assimilated you to be a combination of both without the goofy cape?" Kate said. "You're not quite like the mild-mannered reporter or the caped crusader, although you do fit the bill for playboy Bruce Wayne!" Kate couldn't stop laughing, and neither could Kyle.

"See what you created, Harry; we can work with you or against you." Kyle said.

"Okay, let's just say *we* are," Harry said. "And we are both incognito."

"We," Kate said. "Then Carlita is?"

"Maybe."

"Wait,—hold that thought," Harry said. He ran into his office and came back with a metal object tucked under his arm. It had an ambient glow as the sun bounced off it. He handed it to Kate.

"Oh, my god!" she yelled at the top of her lungs. "It's the da Vinci dream bank."

"Yes, I think you both need this more than I do now," Harry said. "It's the key to your future. Don't lose it."

"This is so cool, Harry," Kate said. "Are you sure we can have it?"

"You bet."

Kate tucked the dream bank tightly under her right arm, and the three of them walked up to the locked gate. She opened the dream bank and noticed it had a dusty old slip of paper inside it with a diagram titled, *'Time Travel.'* She whispered to Kyle, "Harry forgot to take this diagram out of the dream bank." She showed it to Kyle.

"Maybe the diagram is da Vinci's diagram," Kate said. She closed the dream bank back up. "What should we wish for, Kyle?" she said in her regular voice.

"No wishful thinking," Harry said. "Remember, *'Life is a magical opportunity, but you have to create the magic!'*"

"Spoken like a true cyborg!" Kate said. And we experienced our magic today."

"You did, and you took action. But you can't just wish for a dream to come true. As you have seen, you have to set your dream in motion and get to work. The dream bank is a powerful tool to help you do that."

"What if we want to go back to our old lives? Can the dream bank help with that?" Kyle asked.

"It doesn't work that way, son. There's no going back to your old life," Harry said. "Give it time. You're still wet behind the ears. Remember, you have to learn to walk before you can run. One more thing. Now that you know about smart choppers and all their secrets, I can't let you leave quite yet," Harry said.

Scared, the twins slowly turned around to look at Harry. They were ready to fight if need be with their new superhero skills.

"A lot of kids come snooping around here and fall victim to the allure of the cool helicopters," he said. "Just like you two, they have an insatiable appetite for learning about them. What kid doesn't dream about being a pilot or a superhero sometime in his or her childhood? I'll be the first to admit, none of them have come as prepared or as persistent as you two. Not many of them know about da Vinci as well as you do, and very few are let in. The ones who get this magical experience are changed for life. But before you can leave, you must meet the challenge."

"And what might that be?" Kate asked, her arms folded.

"You must promise never to reveal this location or what you saw today. I like the idea that I can help people all around the world and not be chased by the paparazzi. If you do go blabbing to the world then you'll risk losing your empowerment."

"If by chance you do reveal any of my secrets to anyone outside the club you will immediately be banished. I will contact the team and have you eliminated," Harry said with a snicker.

"Yeah right, how are you going to do that?" Kate asked. "We can't die."

"You are surely mistaken as you can die and I hold the key to your life, kid. I have access to secrets I haven't shared with you," Harry said. "Like utilizing magnetic fields and viruses. It's complicated but safer to short-circuit your semiconductors which will neutralize you both. Or I could swap out your brain chips, and you become her and he becomes you." Harry laughed and poked the twins.

"Very funny, Harry," Kate said.

"Well, somebody did come into the hospital room while I dozed and swapped out your chips. We had a hard time booting you to life.

"Okay, Harry," the twins said, looking dejected.

"Sure, Harry," Kyle chuckled. "How do we reach you?" he said.

"I'm just a keystroke away," Harry said. "You can text me. Lastly," he went on, "All the borgs you met today are unique androids with their own magical abilities. All of them are highly trained to catch bullies at a moment's notice. Chantal can find you at thirty thousand feet in the air and surprise you with stinky bird poop when you least expect it. If you're in the water, you might feel the sting of Calypso. The Muscle Men are always looking to get juiced about something. Don't let Huey's age fool you—he has a lot of fight left in him. I don't need to say anything about Sam the Man, the Badass Bros, or Sergeant Major. They speak for themselves when it comes to shock and awe. And don't let Machismo's and Billy Bob's innocence fool you either. So, you have an elite special unit of androids at your disposal if trouble arises. You are part of an elite cyborg team. Be ready when I call and stay dangerous!"

The twins were dumbstruck as Harry unlocked the gate and they walked through.

"Good-bye," Kate said.

Harry winked at her as they turned and walked away.

Kyle and Kate arrived home late for dinner. They immediately sat down at the table, their eyes focused on their mac and cheese. Kate dug in with her fork, their hat and sunglasses on.

"Where have you two been?" Mom said, looking exasperated. "It's dark out. You had us worried. And take off your hats and sunglasses."

Kate looked over at Kyle as Kyle looked at Kate. They hesitated, removed their hats, and went back to eating.

"Excuse me—sunglasses," Mom said.

"We think they are cool and like wearing them, if that is okay with you," Kyle said.

"No, that's not okay. Please remove them," Dad said.

They slowly removed their glasses and looked up.

"Oh my, what happened to you guys?" Mom asked.

"We were at the park, playing with our helicopters when these older kids said it was their park and told us to leave. We didn't, so they punched us in the eye," Kate said.

"But it's okay. As it turned out, this was the best day of our lives!" Kyle chimed in.

"And who are these kids?" Dad asked.

"Will and his girlfriend," Kyle said.

"You want some ice for those eyes?" Dad asked.

"No, we are good," Kyle said.

"Okay then. But next time, come home before dark," their dad said. "Did you still have good time?" He paused, eyeballing them. "And where did you get those jackets and hats? Didn't you both leave in shorts this morning, Kate?"

"Aren't you going to tell them?" Kyle whispered to Kate. "I think we might be in trouble."

Then Mom's face turned to concern, "Tell me what?"

"Well…we were sorta sworn to secrecy," Kyle said, looking at Kate.

"Kyle, stop," Kate whispered.

She looked over at Kyle and winked and he winked back.

"We can't tell you, or something very bad will happen," Kyle said.

"Don't be silly." Mom laughed. "Are there some new mean kids at school? I keep telling you guys you have to stand up to bullies. This isn't the first time you both have come home with black eyes or bloody noses." Mom winked and smirked at Dad.

"Why the wink and smile, we got beat up today by bullies that were bigger than us," Kyle said.

"Sorry, kids. That was insensitive of us. Go on."

"Mom's right," Kate whispered to Kyle. "What are we scared of? We're superheroes!"

"Well, alright…" Kyle said. "We had this incredible day of adventure. We met this superhero, and he showed us everything about helicopters. And he made us superheroes."

Mom and Dad winked at each other and smirked again.

Mom laughed. "Superheroes!"

"We didn't get to take the final exam, but it's the last stage to becoming superhero cyborgs," Kyle said.

Mom and Dad looked at each.

"Anyway, the pilot we met crashed his chopper into a huge ball of flames, and he can fly with hand propellers. He gave us his da Vinci dream bank from when he went time-traveling into a black hole and met Leonardo Da Vinci," Kyle continued.

"Yeah, and we met a dog named Borg and Poo Daddy, the bear that can fly a chopper," Kate said. "And we flew to Lake Tahoe and the Gulf Coast and met Jackaroo from Australia."

Mom laughed. "Poo Daddy, and Jackaroo. That's a good one, 2500 miles each way in a helicopter in one day. You must have been flying at the speed of light!"

"Oh, my god," Kate whispered to Kyle. "We didn't fly at 186,000 miles per second did we?"

"Could Turbo have been running on pumpkin biofuel?" Kyle asked.

"And remember the TT lever that Harry said was nothing? Maybe it stood for Turbo Time or time travel. " Kate said.

"Wait a second. My onboard computer is calcualating today's speed and time. We traveled at the speed of light which is why we got so much accomplished in one day." Kyle said.

"Oy my god," Kate whispered to him.

"Did some strange man really give you something? Let me see it!" Mom interrupted.

Kate pulled the dream bank out from under the table and handed it to Mom, exposing her tattoo.

"This looks valuable," Mom said, looking it over. "What are these papers inside? This thing looks like an artifact from the days of antiquity. Where did you guys really get this? I'm going to hold onto it."

Just then, the lid closed tightly, pinching her finger. The dream bank began to vibrate violently. It fell from Mom's hand to the floor with a clang and rolled to a stop at Kate's foot. Kate picked it up and set it on the table next to her.

"What just happened?" Mom asked. "Is da Vinci going to pop out of the genie bottle now?" Mom and Dad laughed.

"Um,—you woke up the magical forces that can unlock the universe's secrets to make dreams come true?" Kate said.

"Or you really pissed it off and now it's going to kill all of us!" Kyle said. He poked Kate and they both laughed.

"Anyway, you can't keep our dream bank," Kate said.

"You just watch me, young lady! Who really gave you this, what's this superhero's name?"

Kyle turned to Kate and whispered, "She's a nonbeliever. The dream bank picked up her negative energy."

"Oh, my god," Kate whispered back.

"Is that a tattoo on your wrist? Didn't we discuss that tattoos were forbidden until you turn eighteen?" Mom said.

"Yes, but these tattoos are different in that they hold secret powers," Kate said.

"I see, and you will have them removed before you go back to school," Dad said.

"No way, they can't be removed," Kyle said.

"Yes, way. And you went swimming today?" Dad questioned.

"Yeah, we were with Captain Calypso and I wasn't clipped in when we went to rescue a family. And I fell into the ocean and Kyle jumped in to save me, and we both drowned. It's a long story, we don't want to bore you," Kate said.

"Please bore us!"

"Okay, we died and were rebuilt into cyborgs. We can fly with our hand propellers," Kyle said.

"You did what?" Dad exclaimed and looked at Mom with surprise. Mom glared back at Dad. "What's this superhero's name, and where is this place?"

"He calls himself Helicopter Harry," Kate said. He is a cyborg but we think he is Prince Harry. We can't tell you where his heliport is."

"Helicopter Harry, what kind of name is that?" Mom laughed. "Some cyborg superhero out of your action-hero comic books? Keep dreaming, kids!"

"That's what Harry said too, keep dreaming." The twins leaned into each other, nudged shoulders and laughed.

"Yeah, right," Mom laughed and snorted. "You met Prince Harry, and he is a cyborg named Helicopter Harry." Mom laughed. "Is there such a thing?"

"Here we go again with comic-book mind manipulation." Mom snorted and laughed. She winked at Dad and Dad winked back at her.

Kate whispered to Kyle. "Why are Mom and Dad winking so much?"

"I don't know. Did we say something funny?"

"For the last time, didn't I tell you you're *not* going to be fancy schmancy pilots, let alone glamorous superheroes? Look, young lady; you're going to make a wonderful attorney, like me, and your brother will make a fine engineer like your father," Mom said.

Both kids looked at each other and mouthed, *"Not."* They stuck their fingers in their mouths and pretended to gag like Carlita did. Mom and Dad laughed. Then Mom and Dad did the same thing.

"You're making fun of us!" Kate said.

Dad looked at Mom and said, "Honey, don't you think we should tell them now before this goes any further?"

"What are you talking about?" Kate demanded.

"I suppose, we've had our fun," Mom said. "Maybe scared you too!" She chuckled.

Both kids looked surprised and confused.

"What the—" Kyle said.

"You want to tell them or should I?" Mom said to Dad.

"Congratulations, you made it through bootcamp!" Mom said. "We were not looking forward to this day. I did not want you to become cyborgs."

The twins' mouths dropped open.

"What did you say, Mom?" Kate mumbled.

"We knew this day would come, so we tried to steer you in another direction, to make being an attorney and an engineer sound as exciting as possible," Dad said.

"Okay. I'm lost," Kate said.

"Me too." Kyle said. "Are you really a nuclear engineer?" Kyle hesitantly asked.

"Yes, I am," Dad said.

"What. Really?" Kyle said. "And you build rockets for SpaceX?"

"Yeah, for Big E," Dad said.

"Go figure," Kyle said. "Is he a cyborg too?"

"You have to ask?" Dad said.

"We know Harry and called him to keep an eye on you in the park," Mom said. "But then he crashed his helicopter and changed everything. He was supposed to just circle around you, and let us know you were okay."

"What? Oh my god!" Kate said.

"If you know Harry, does this mean you are superhero cyborgs?" Kate said.

"Yes, honey, we are cyborgs. We were both killed in a car accident when you were just two years old. Harry was chasing a trouble-making cyborg which caused us to crash when a cyborg flew through our windshield and killed us," Mom said. "Do you remember anything about that crash?"

"Nothing," Kate said.

"Wow, sorta like how Will flew into Calypso and caused us to die. Was it Will that killed you both?" Kyle said.

"No, it was his parents. Harry felt bad and saved us like Calypso saved you when Will hit your helicopter and knocked you into the water," Dad said. "We watched you drown on our big-screen TV as Calypso relayed the live video feed through her Bluetooth," Dad said.

"Oh mu god," Kate said. "Really?"

"I'm proud of you both," Mom said. "We have our cover identities as an attorney and an engineer but we still help Harry eliminate bad guys from time to time. We are highly trained assassins. It's not just humans that are crazy, it's cyborgs and androids too! We are here to keep them all in line."

Kate interrupted, "Oh my god, I can't believe this!"

"Yeah, I'm blown away," Kyle said.

"Listen, you're going to carry on with your lives just like us. Go to school. No beating up bullies unless you need to defend yourselves, and keep the hand rotors hidden. I give you permission to dole out the occasional black eye and bloody nose if the situation merits it. Your classmates do not need to know you are superheroes— yet. We come out of our human shells only when we are called to duty," Dad said.

"Yes, Dad, Harry informed us to stay under the radar as cyborgs and act as humanly as possible," Kate said.

"We wish this wasn't the case but it is. Just think, no silly capes but hand rotors," Mom said.

"You guys have hand rotors too?" Kyle said.

"Yes, but even though we have cyborg capabilities, we are still quite human." Dad pulled up his sleeve and showed his tattoo like theirs. "We are truly united now."

"Oy my god, Mom, I can't believe you didn't tell us this before," Kate said.

"Like I said, I wanted you to stay human for as long as possible, if indefinitely. Now, I think that is enough for tonight. Off to bed, "Mom said. "One more thing. Here is your dream bank. I think it helped you accomplish your dreams. It snapped at me because I wasn't ready for you to be who you've become. Treasure it," Mom said.

"We are over-loaded and could use some rest after the day we've had," Kate said.

"And please pick up your stack of comic books by the stairs and take them to your room before someone trips over them," Mom said.

"Okay, love you guys," Kyle said

"Back at you, kiddo," Dad said.

Kyle gathered the comic books but tripped as he neared the top stair. He dropped them, and they slid down to the bottom. He walked down, gathered them up, and noticed something unusual about one of them. It was titled, *Helicopter Harry.* He screamed and dropped the comic book.

"What's your problem?" Kate asked. As she picked up the comic book, she screamed too. "What the, where did this come from?" she asked.

"Don't open it," Kyle said.

"Just the first page," she shrieked! "Oh, my god! How can this be?"

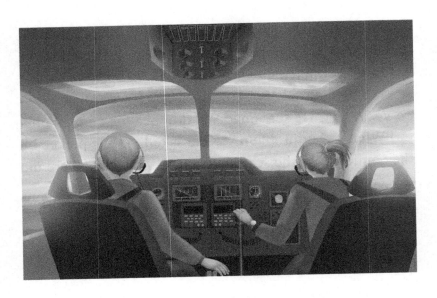

DREAM It, LEARN It, DO It!

Take a chance and live your dream!

A s The twins slept that night, their minds drifted into dreams in which they were superheroes. In one of the dreams, Kate received a text from Harry on her smartphone.

"Hello, Kate," Harry said. "I have a mission for you and Kyle. Are you available now?"

"Sure, Prince Charming. What's up?" Kate texted back.

"The Tower of Power in San Francisco is on fire because Will launched an attack into it. The tower is ablaze and is threatening the safety of everyone in the city. This tower processes pumpkin biomass into biofuel and is currently storing thousands of tons. If it were to blow, it would level the city and we would be knee-deep in orange slime."

The Tower of Power is orange and looks like a regular skyscraper although it's as wide as a city block.

"Wow, Harry. Sounds like a stinky situation." Kate chuckled. "What do you want us to do?"

"I'll meet you and Kyle at the heliport for a briefing," Harry told her.

Kate ran out to Kyle in the backyard and shouted, "Hey, Harry has a mission for us! A chopper crashed into the Tower of Power in San Francisco, and it's on fire. Do you think we can do it?"

"Heck, yeah," Kyle said proudly. "We're superheroes, aren't we?"

They grabbed their bikes from the garage and sped off excitedly.

Before they got very far, Kyle slammed on his brakes and skidded to a stop. "Where's your flight jacket, Kate?"

She looked surprised. "I don't know."

"Where did you have it last?" Kyle said.

"Maybe we don't need them, now that we are cyborgs?" Kate said.

"Let's not take a chance. Go find it," Kyle said. "And besides, we look cool in them."

"It was in my closet," she said. "But it wasn't there the last time I looked."

Picturing her closet with clothes strewn everywhere, Kyle laughed. "Maybe Mom's washing it with your dirty underpants?" He laughed again and nudged her on the shoulder. "Gross!"

"Oh my God, you can't wash the flight jackets!" Kate wailed.

"Better go find it if you're going to fly today," he said. "Or maybe you're not going to fly today?"

"No way, dude. I'll be right back!"

Kate rode home, dropped her bike at the front door, and raced upstairs into the bedroom. She nearly tore it apart looking for the flight jacket. She looked in the closet again. "Not on the floor," she said to herself. She looked in the hamper full of dirty underpants. She checked the bathroom. No jacket.

She remembered Harry telling her not to lose the jacket because she couldn't fly without it. Tears welled up in her eyes and then streamed down her face as she threw herself onto her bed and stared at the ceiling. Her mind raced as she looked at the closet and locked onto something. She jumped to her feet, wiped her eyes, and saw a yellow raincoat covering up her flight jacket, which was hanging neatly on a hanger. She then remembered covering it up to disguise it so no one would find it—apparently not even her. She jerked off the raincoat, tossed it to the floor, and grabbed the flight jacket. Putting it on, she raced back downstairs, losing her balance and bouncing off the wall in her excitement. She ran outside to Kyle, feeling even more empowered. She yelled, "I found it!"

"Where was it?" Kyle asked.

"Right where it was supposed to be," she replied.

"Brain fart!" Kyle joked.

The twins raced their bikes as fast as they could to the heliport. Once they arrived, they dropped their bikes at the gate and met Harry, who buzzed them in.

"Glad you could make it, kids," he said. "We have a situation on our hands. Kate, you take Helicopter Huey. Pick up the attorneys and engineers who are stranded on the tower and bring them to an adjacent tower for safety."

"Attorneys and engineers? You're joking!" Kate exclaimed.

Harry shrugged. "Yeah, how ironic. Maybe there's a lesson to be learned, kid. Kyle, I need you and Fiona to put out the fire. Poo Daddy will join you as your wing-man in his new chopper. And I'll fly over to the tower and check on it. If Will is anywhere to be seen, I'll let you know," Harry said.

"This is truly your baptism by fire," he continued. "If you successfully complete this mission without getting hurt or killed, you'll move onto the next level."

"Come on, Harry, we can't be killed," Kate said.

"Oh yes you can. Will can trap you in a magnetic field and short-circuit you and there is no bringing you back. You are gone forever!" Harry said.

"Does the next level include more combat with shock and awe?" Kyle asked.

"Possibly," Harry said, wiggling an eyebrow.

"Boy, I hope so," Kate said. "Maybe we'll see Will again!"

"He is bigger and stronger than both of you," Harry said.

"And doesn't going Kommando mean not wearing underpants?" Kate said.

"Yup, and he is a sick twit, as you know!" Harry said.

"So we could pants him, embarrass him, and maybe kill him?" Kyle said.

"Keep dreaming, kid."

Kate ran over to Helicopter Huey and gave him a slap on the front.

"Yo, yo, yo, it's about time you got here." Huey fluttered his eyes. "We're behind schedule, and lives are depending on you. Don't screw this up, kid!"

"Okay, tough guy, we're just kids," Kate said. She rubbed the nose of the chopper with love. "We can only pedal our bikes so fast. It's not like we can drive a car!" she added, laughing.

"That's not what I heard," Huey said with a smirk.

Kate fired up Helicopter Huey with a turn of a key and the push of a button, which made the engine sputter with black smoke. Kate rolled on the throttle and pulled up on the collective as they lifted off the ground.

"Are you sure you're up for this, old fart?" Kate joked.

Huey fluttered his eyes again with a stern look. "This old fart can beat you young punks any day! Maybe A-Star was right, and you're too smart for your britches! Now, I need to stretch this old rotor. Let's get on with it."

"Wow, aren't you sensitive today?" Kate said.

"I didn't sleep well last night. I had a lot of gas so I'm a little cranky."

As they approached downtown San Francisco, Kate saw the burning tower with the attorneys and engineers waving for help on the balcony.

Black smoke filled the sky, and Kate saw Harry flying around the burning building trying to locate Will. Harry then landed on top of the building.

"Surprise," Carlita said, as she landed on top of the building as well.

"Glad you could join the party," Harry said.

"Do you see Will?" Carlita asked.

"That's a negative. Looks like he has slipped away. There goes Kate, let's get out of her way."

"Kate, I hope you're feeling empowered. As I said, people are depending on you," Huey said.

"I'll do my best," she said.

Kate nervously wiped a bead of sweat from her brow. She then took a pass around the building, checking out the people who needed to be rescued.

"Who would have thought I'd be saving attorneys and engineers?" Kate joked. "Rescuing these clowns isn't superhero stuff. I should be chasing Will! Look at them, all dolled up in their fancy business suits," Kate said.

"Move in closer so a few people can climb into the basket," Huey said. "Closer, closer, closer, perfect! Okay, they're in. Let's swing over to the other building and drop them off."

"Ten-four, Huey." Kate positioned Huey over the other tower, where the rescue staff was waiting.

"Great job, Kate," Huey said. "You're a natural. Just keep the chopper steady as the people exit the basket."

After the first batch of engineers and attorneys were safely on the other tower, Kate and Huey headed for another load of people. As they did, they saw Kyle and Poo Daddy making water drops on the building.

Kate radioed Kyle. "How's it going with the water drops?"

"Well, I don't know if I'm making a dent in the fire. It seems to be out of control and spreading to other buildings. I'm going to radio for backup. Have you heard from Harry?"

"Not lately. Last I heard, he and Carlita had landed on the building to see if Will was still around," Kate said.

"I wonder if he needs our help."

"We have our own problems right now," Kate told him. "Let's stay on task here."

"Okay, sis," Kyle said. Then he radioed to Muscle and Viktor for help.

Kate was hovering as the last of the people exited the basket. Suddenly, the emergency horn came on.

Startled, she looked at the gas gauge. "Oh man! I thought you got gas before we took off, Huey!"

"I am full of gas but not the right kind. And I thought *you* did. You're the pilot!" Huey said, frowning. "Wow, no gas. This isn't good."

"Sorry, another brain fart!" Kate said. "Now we're going to crash and burn after we rescued all those people."

"Wait a minute!" Huey shouted. "I just remembered. There should be a gallon of gas left in reserve, which means we have about five more minutes of flight time!"

A wave of relief swept over Kate as her eyes welled up. She wiped away a tear. "Do you think we'll make it?" she cried.

"Cheer up, kid. We'll just do an autorotation to the ground," he said. "If not, engage your hand rotors as you jump from the chopper, and say, *"Hasta la vista, baby!"*

"Thanks for reminding me of how Kyle and I first met Harry," she said, visualizing the burning chopper. "I don't see any place to land—only buildings, the freeway, and a whole lot of water." Kate's heart sank as she recalled drowning.

She was racing at two hundred miles an hour, watching the gas gauge and the clock. *TICK, TOCK, TICK, TOCK.*

"Don't you think we should slow down and conserve gas?" Huey asked.

"No way, dude," she replied. "Because if we do crash land, we won't have so far to walk back to the heliport."

Then she saw a flash. Will flew in front of the windshield and pointed at her.

"You're going to *die*!" he said. He flew into the chopper and tried to make them crash. Then he flew off.

"Oh my god, don't you dare crash me," Huey pleaded. "I don't wanna die like Hank!" Huey visualized the burning chopper that Harry had crashed. "He's toying with you, Kate."

"I don't want to die either, Huey!" Kate said. "Kyle and I have to make it to the next level. Hold on, Huey. I set the autopilot. Just hover here for a quick moment, This bully needs to taste my rockets!"

"Make it quick, we don't have much time." Little beads of sweat were forming on the windshield.

"Don't *you* ever try to bully me again!" Kate yelled through the loudspeaker. She opened the door and jumped out, engaged her hand rotors and flew within fifty feet of him.

"Show me what you got, punk!" Will said.

Kate fired a rocket from each arm, which made a loud explosion, and sent him to the ground in a ball of flames.

She felt relieved that she might have killed Will. She flew back into Huey and sat down. "Okay, I'm back." She flicked the wiper blades as she spotted the heliport about a mile ahead.

"Nice job, Kate," Huey said. "And not much time to spare."

"We're coming in," she radioed, "but I don't think we have enough gas to land!" Just as she finished her sentence, the motor quit, and she got a sinking feeling in her stomach.

"Don't panic Kate. You'll be fine," Machismo encouraged her from the heliport. "Remember your ABCs, Kate!" he urged her, as she started to cry. "Cyborgs don't cry. And you know *B* for brave!"

"I don't know, Will has me really scared."

"C!" Machismo yelled. "Stay cool, calm and collected!"

"I do look pretty cool in Helicopter Huey, don't I, Machismo?" Kate said, trying to smile.

"That's not what I mean!" Machismo said.

"Turn down that blasted emergency warning, would you, Huey?" Kate cried as the recording came on. *PREPARE TO DIE, PREPARE TO DIE, PREPARE TO DIE…*

She gave it a slap, and it stopped.

"Okay, I have a grip!" she said confidently. With her eyes wide open, she added, "I'm ready to autorotate now."

She wiped her eyes with her hand.

Helicopter Huey had a frightened look on his face and couldn't watch anymore. He shut his eyes as they approached the heliport. His rotor turned with a slow *WHOOPH, WHOOPH, WHOOPH.*

"I'm good to go," Kate called out as the heliport came into view. Her mind was clear and focused.

All the choppers on the ground turned and centered their attention on Kate. Anxious cheers erupted as everyone nervously waited in anticipation.

"You don't have any room for error, Kate," Machismo announced. "Easy, Kate. You're doing fine. Now gently pull back on the cyclic stick, and ease down the collective. Keep the nose up, and set Huey down on the ground."

The helicopter skid-bounced on the tarmac and back into the air.

"What do I do, Machismo?" Kate visualized Harry's burning chopper again.

"Focus on the task at hand!" he said. "Ease her down."

The chopper slammed down on the ground and slid sideways, rocking to the left like it was going to fall on its side. Then it rocked to the right, teetered on the skid, and fell over. Kate was knocked unconscious but soon woke up to the voice of Machismo on the loudspeaker, *"He's gonna blow, Kate, get out!"* She was strapped into the helicopter. She struggled to unbuckle herself as quickly as possible, then climbed out.

Machismo announced, "Just kidding, and congratulations, Kate! You did it—well, not exactly as planned, but you did it." All the choppers on the tarmac scurried around and slapped rotors with one another.

"Not without knowing my ABCs," Kate said. I hope Helicopter Huey is okay."

"He's fine," Machismo said. "You wouldn't know it, but he's back to getting his beauty sleep from all the excitement you created. Remember this day when you get yourself in a tight spot. You almost forgot your ABCs in all the excitement, which could have become deadly."

"You're right, Machismo," Kate said. "I'll never forget them again."

Meanwhile, the tower fire raged on. Kyle and Poo Daddy did their best to put out the flames along with the small fires in the surrounding office buildings.

Kyle radioed his wingman. "Hey, Poo Daddy, it looks like the fire has spread to the zoo. Do you think you can maneuver in to put it out?

"You bet," Poo Daddy replied.

"Ten-four," Kyle said. "You're on your own. Talk to me when you have the situation under control."

Poo Daddy dropped away. "You got it, Kyle," he called out.

"Backup has arrived!" Fiona shouted, "Sergeant Major, Muscle, and Vertical Viktor are swooping into the San Francisco Bay to pick up water."

"Awesome," Kyle said. "We might tame this beast sooner than expected! "Hey, Muscle," Kyle radioed. "Glad to see you could join the party."

"I wouldn't miss it," Muscle said. "We need to *terminate* this fire *now*!"

Sergeant Major clicked in. "Knock off all the jawing, boys! What do you say we corral this fire? I'll come in from the north. Kyle, you and Fiona come in from the east, and Muscle and Viktor will take the west and south. Once we're in place, we'll have a ring around the fire. And then we'll put this bad boy out once and for all!"

"Sounds like a plan," Kyle replied.

"Hey," Fiona shouted. "I'm overheating, and it's not from the dang fire! Steam is coming out of my engine compartment."

"Are you going to be alright?" Kyle asked. "Do we need to set down and rest your old bolts?"

"I have a better idea. I'm going to swing underneath Muscle. As he releases his bucket of water, I can cool down."

"Great idea, Fiona," Muscle said.

"Has anyone heard from Poo Daddy? Don't you think he should have checked in by now?" Kyle asked. He radioed Poo Daddy. "Kyle to Poo Daddy. Do you read me?"

A long silence followed.

"Poo Daddy, it's Kyle. Where are you?"

"Do you think he crashed?" Viktor asked. "Maybe Will got to him?"

"I doubt it," Muscle radioed back.

"Hey, Muscle, let me swing under you for that shower," Fiona said.

"Go for it, little lady," Muscle replied.

Kyle slid Fiona underneath Muscle so she could get doused from above.

"Wow!" Fiona said with a smile. "Thanks, Kyle. That did the trick. I'm way cool now."

"Oh, my god, there's Poo Daddy's chopper," Kyle said, pointing to the ground. "It looks like a crumpled aluminum can with smoke seeping out of it. I'm going to land and look for Poo Daddy."

"Go for it, kid," Sergeant Major said. "We got a handle on the fire. Wow, that's the second chopper he has crashed."

Everyone was sad because they feared the worst for Poo Daddy. Kyle landed and looked for Poo Daddy in the Copter Cub. He peeked inside and shouted into his headset, "Poo Daddy isn't here. What do you think happened?"

"Maybe somebody dragged him off," Fiona replied.

"Do you hear that?" Kyle asked. "I hear the faint sound of a harmonica coming from the zoo just a block away."

Fiona's ears perked up as Kyle walked over to check it out. To his surprise, he saw Poo Daddy with some other bears.

"Hey, Poo Daddy. Is that you?" Kyle called out.

Poo Daddy stopped playing his harmonica, and the bears froze in place. He then lowered his sunglasses to the edge of his nose. They looked over at Kyle and dropped to all fours.

"Hi, Kyle," Poo Daddy said with a wave, and pushed his glasses back up.

"What the heck is going on?" asked Kyle.

"We're having a party," Poo Daddy replied. "The zoo was a raging inferno, but I was able to put it out. We'll these bears saved me when I crashed."

"I can't believe you're alive!"

"Who's your daddy!" Poo Daddy said. "The bears pulled me out of the chopper, and they then smothered me with love. Turns out the mama bear was a friend of my mom's, may she rest in peace. They refused to be bullied by this fire, let alone hunters. And they have a message for all the hunters out there too: We might surprise you in the woods one night, and it ain't going to be pretty when we poke our heads into your tents at three in the morning and yell, *'Fire!' and watch you try to get out of your sleeping bags and then eat you!"* Kyle and the bears erupted so hard into laughter that their stomachs hurt.

"Would you like a s'more? We're roasting them over what's left of the fire," Poo Daddy said.

"You bet," Kyle said. "That sure looks good right now."

"Fire *terminated*!" Muscle cheered on the radio. "We're all pretty beat, so we're heading back to base."

"Okay, Muscle," Kyle said. "Has anyone talked to Harry?"

"No, we haven't heard from him," Muscle said.

"Okay, I'll check on him," Kyle replied. "By the way, I found Poo Daddy, and he's alive!"

Muscle cheered back, "Yeah! We can't lose the world's one and only firefighting bear. See y'all later."

"How many buckets of water did it take to save the bears, Poo Daddy?" Kyle asked.

"Boy, what a hustle that was," Poo Daddy said. "The flames were licking at my chopper with a vengeance. It made me wonder if I was going to save the zoo. I stopped counting my water drops as I got light-headed from the heat. I felt a thump against the chopper, blacked out and crashed. The next thing I knew, I was in this dream state as the bears dragged me to safety."

"You felt a thump but you didn't see Will," Kate said.

"Nope, but I did see a purple flash wiz by."

"Who's your daddy!" Kyle said with excitement.

"Poo Daddy, that's who!" Kate said. "I don't know any other firefighting bear that would put his life on the line, let alone fly a chopper into the path of danger."

Kyle radioed Harry to make contact. "Harry, do you read me?"

"Yes, Kyle, loud and clear."

"Is everything okay?" Kate said.

"No, Will is nowhere to be seen," Harry said.

"I think he caused Poo Daddy to crash with his signature thump into the side of the chopper," Kate said.

"Great job today, Kyle. We couldn't have done it without you."

"Did we make it to the next level?" Kate asked.

The twins suddenly woke up. They sat up in their bunk beds, looking at each other with their flight jackets on.

"I just had this wild dream about flying Helicopter Huey," Kate said.

"I had a dream that I was flying Fiona!" Kyle said. "And it felt incredibly real. A chopper crashed into the Tower of Power and set it ablaze. And of all things, you were rescuing attorneys and engineers from the rooftop as I fought the fire."

"That's too weird!" Kate said. "I had the same exact dream."

"I sure feel empowered as a superhero now," Kyle said.

Kate nodded. "Yeah, me too. Maybe we should help Harry save the tower from the bullies."

"Maybe we should sleep on it," Kyle said.

"Yeah, but I think now is the right time. Remember the code? *Dream It, Learn It, Do It!* Well, we dreamed of being superheroes and we learned it, so let's *do it*!" she said excitedly.

"So you're saying we should steal a helicopter?" Kyle asked. "Do we even need one when we have hand rotors?"

"We need Turbo because we figured out that he is the time machine all along and it offers us better protection against Will. Sorta like a coat of amour. But I wouldn't call it stealing ," Kate said. "More like borrowing, like when we took Mom's car out."

"Oh, man, I hope you know what you're doing, Kate. I don't want Sam the Man to put us in jail."

"You watch, Sam is a pushover. He has a loud bark but no bite."

"Okay, Kate," Kyle said with hesitation. "But let's do a pinky swear that nothing goes wrong!"

They locked pinkies and tugged hard.

"Let's get going, and maybe we can get back before Mom and Dad wake up in the morning and then we'll make them proud," Kate said. "Should we fly with our hand rotors?"

"No, too dark, can't see the power lines," Kyle said.

The twins flew out of their bunk beds, scrambled to change their clothes, and climbed out the window. They grabbed their bikes and raced to the heliport. It was pitch-black outside, and they had a hard time seeing. Kate didn't notice a large plastic trash can in her path and slammed into it. She flew over the handlebars, hit the pavement, and rolled to a stop. Her palms and knees were scraped and tiny pieces of gravel were stuck to her skin.

"Oh, my god!" she groaned. A tear dropped from the corner of her eye. Before she had a chance to really cry, Kyle rode up. "Are you okay, sis?" He laid his bike down and began to console her with an arm around her shoulder.

"I'm okay, but I think I wet my underpants." She held back tears of pain as she wiped her hands on her pants.

"Are you crying?"

"Yeah, maybe a little."

"Cyborgs don't cry. Let me see your hand and knee."

Kate showed him her hand. "There is nothing wrong with your hand or knee and you didn't wet yourself. You have subdermal titanium skin. It's puncture-proof. Just wipe away the pebbles that are stuck on the skin."

"I guess I had a human reaction, and I was shaken up a little."

"That's because your cyborg brain hasn't completely uploaded yet. Okay? What are you waiting for?" Kyle asked, "Get back on your bike, and let's go. We don't have much time."

Kate walked over to her bike, lifted it up, and got back on it. But she couldn't pedal it because the front wheel was bent and was rubbing against the fork. Her mood changed from inconsolable to mad as heck.

"What do we do now, Kyle?" she shouted.

"First, remember the three Cs," Kyle said, laughing.

"Kyle!" Kate said, raising her voice.

"Maybe we should go back home and try another time."

"No way, dude! We did a pinky swear and this is just a bump in the road. We've come this far, and we're not going back. Lift up the trash can and help me put the bike in it."

They each grabbed a wheel of the bike, and Kate lowered the front of the bike into the trash can as Kyle gently lowered the rest of it in.

"Are you going to walk?" Kyle asked.

"Heck, no," she said. "We're both going on your bike! I'll sit on the handlebars, and you pedal."

Kate developed a strategy to stop them from hitting any more trash cans. She held onto the bars, with her feet pointing straight out in front of her and kicked each can aside. They rode and wobbled back and forth down the road until they reached the heliport. There weren't any lights on at the heliport, which made The twins uneasy. Kyle stashed his bike in the bushes near the fence and he and Kate walked down the fence line, looking for the gate. As soon as they found it, they looked up at the eye scanner, but they weren't tall enough to look directly into it. Each of them jumped as high as they could, but it wasn't high enough.

"This is madness," Kyle said. "Just climb up the fence, Kate, look into the scanner and get us in."

She shook her head. "No way. The fence might be electrified. Remember what Harry said? When nobody is here, they turn the fence on. Why don't you touch the fence, and see? We don't have time for this. Be brave, like Billy Bob said."

"What's brave about touching fifty thousand volts?" Kyle said.

"It's not like it's going to hurt." Kate broke into laughter and slapped Kyle on the back.

"I have a better idea. Get on my shoulders. I think you'll be able to reach the eye scanner that way."

She climbed onto Kyle's shoulders and looked into the scanner.

"Stand on your tiptoes, Kyle!" She was holding on with both hands over Kyle's forehead as she wobbled back and forth. Her hands slipped over his eyes. Kyle grabbed the fence to stabilize himself. He immediately felt fifty-thousand volts of electricity sear through his body and into Kate's.

"Okay, what just happened?" Kate asked. "My body vibrated from head to toe, which felt pretty cool."

"First of all, you're not dead. Secondly, that's what fifty-thousand volts of electricity feels like."

"That wasn't so bad. My mind is more clear."

"Okay, I *am* on my tiptoes!" Kyle said. "But get your hands off my eyes."

"Gross, did you fart?" Kyle said, laughing hysterically.

Kate laughed too. "Maybe a little. It's from the mac and cheese Mom made last night. Hey, the eye scanner isn't working, it's still red," she said, "I'm squinting into it and nothing!"

"Maybe it's set for my eyes," Kyle said. "Let me get on your shoulders, Kate." He snickered.

The two switched places. Kyle stood on Kate's shoulders and looked into the eye scanner. The lights turned green and the gate latch clicked open. Kyle quietly pushed open the gate as he got off Kate, and they looked at each other nervously. Kyle began to speak just as Kate put her forefinger over his lips. Although he couldn't see her face because it was so dark, they froze at the gate. It was so quiet that they could only hear their hearts pounding against their chests. Then, all of sudden....a voice!

"Who goes there? You're about to get tasered!" It was Sam the Man yelling. The twins just about jumped out of their skins as his floodlight silhouetted their little bodies.

"It's just us, Sam," Kate said. "Kate and Kyle."

Sam turned the floodlight away. "You had me scared there for a moment."

"Back at you, S-Sam," Kyle stuttered, fearing going to jail.

"What are you two doing here?" Sam asked. "It's late."

"We couldn't sleep, so we thought we'd come down and mosey around," Kate said.

"I don't know what you guys are up to, but Harry said you could be trusted," Sam said. "I got a text from him earlier, boasting about your mission with Windmaker and Striker. As hard as this is to say, you made me proud. Anyway, knock yourselves out, but remember not to wake Huey. Turn out the lights and lock up when you leave."

"Sam, there aren't any lights," Kyle said. "I just have this little flashlight that barely works."

"Oh, right," Sam said. "I meant to lock the gate when you leave."

"Sure, Sam. Whatever you say," Kate said.

"One more thing," Sam said. "Did you hear about Harry?"

"No, what are you talking about?" Kate asked.

"Will tricked Harry and may have fried him with a magnetic field. Harry was trying to save Britain's supply of pumpkin biofuel but fell into Will's trap. Will pretended to be Carlita in disguise. You know how he tried to level San Francisco? Well, he wants to blow up the factory in Britain and level that place too." He's mad at the whole world."

"Oh my god, are you serious?" Kyle said.

"So—Harry is feared dead. You can't come back from the magnetic field."

"Are you sure?" Kate asked.

"There is a way, but one of you would have to sacrifice yourself by trading places with Harry."

Kate said, "Holy shish kebab! Unbelievable!" She began to tremble, and her voice broke. "Dead, dead?"

"I'm sorry," Sam said. "I thought you'd heard. We don't know for sure that he's dead, but our crew always expects the worst since we have hearts of hardened steel. It's just a wait-and-see situation."

"Thanks, Sam," Kyle said.

The twins started to walk away. Kyle fumbled with his flashlight and Kate wiped away a tear.

"Does Carlita know?" Kate asked, turning back to Sam.

"No, I haven't had the heart to tell her. She thinks the world of him. If there ever was a perfect couple. Sorry, I'm rambling, Kate. Meghan—I mean Carlita—knows Harry's on a secret mission and might be the only one that can save him, if he is alive, of course. Do you think you can let *her* know and then get back to me? You should see them fly together with their outstretched arms. They are such a dynamic duo!"

"Okay, Sam. I'll call or text her." Kate said, wondering how she would break the news to her new friend.

"I don't know, Kate. I have a bad feeling about this. It felt like Harry was passing down his legacy when he gave us his dream bank. He sorta talked like he wasn't going to see us anymore," said Kyle.

"Yeah, I know," Kate said.

"Maybe we could use the time machine and prevent whatever tragedy struck," Kyle suggested.

"How are we going to do that? I don't think we have time to do that before Mom and Dad wake up."

"But what if the worst did happen? Who will take over?" Kate said.

"Mom and Dad. But let's not complicate it any more than we need to at the moment," Kate said. "I'm getting overloaded. First things first. We contact Carlita and then find Turbo. Then we have to convince Turbo to help us find Harry. Then we enlist Harry's motley crew of special agents."

"Do you really think the team can perform?" Kyle said.

"Heck, yeah!"

"How is it you think of everything, Kate?" Kyle said. "You're so smart."

Kate shrugged. "Girls are smarter than boys, so, get with the program. We find Turbo and tell him we want to find Harry. Don't say anything about da Vinci. Just follow my lead."

"Okay, Kate. I'll follow your lead. I think I see Turbo over there." Kyle again fumbled with his flashlight, trying to turn it on. He shook it a few times until it lit up, and then he pointed it toward Turbo. "Yeah, there he is."

The kids ran over to Turbo and gently opened his door. They climbed in and sat there, out of breath.

"Hi, guys," Turbo said. "What brings you into my wonderful world tonight?" Turbo's cockpit lights came on, startling the twins. They looked at each other with wide eyes.

"Uh…just a friendly little joyride," Kyle said with a laugh.

Kate tilted her head to the side and gave Kyle the stink eye. "We heard Harry is missing in action, and we need to go find him."

"Yes, young lady. I also heard a rumor to that effect, but you might be wasting your time looking for him," Turbo said.

"Don't worry," Kate told him. "We won't be wasting our time." She winced, holding back a tear. "We'll bring back *Harry.*"

"How are you going to do this? You remember how to fly?" Turbo asked.

"Yes, we do. We feel very empowered at the moment," Kate said.

"Full tank of gas, Turbo?" Kyle asked.

"Yes, and pumpkin biofuel never smelled better," Turbo said with a smile.

"Smells like pumpkin pie, although I don't think I can ever eat pumpkin pie again knowing what I know now," Kate said. "Let's rock!"

Kate gave a twist of the key, and the engine fired up with a rumble. The rotor began to twist around and around, wiping the air at high speed. The twins put on their headsets as Turbo warmed up.

"Okay, Turbo," she said. "Everything looks good."

Kate pulled up on the collective and steadied Turbo with the cyclic stick as Kyle worked the pedals on his side. They lifted off and soared upward toward the glistening stars. With a smile, Kyle pointed to the Big Dipper.

It looked like they could fly right to it. Kate pointed to Venus with the same enthusiasm.

"Hey, look at that shooting star!"

"Make a wish, Kate," Kyle said.

Kate closed her eyes tightly for a second and said, "I wish we find Harry alive!"

"Me too, Kate. Okay, we're approaching ten thousand feet and I don't think we can go much higher."

Then the twins heard a loud thud. Something had hit the side of the chopper.

"What was that?" Kate said.

"I think it's Will," Kyle said.

"We have to get into the hyper-loop to shake him off," Kate said.

"Ten-four, Kate, Kyle said. "Turbo, we need those turbos now for our hyper-loop, and we have to shake Will loose."

"Are you sure you know what you're doing, Kate?" Kyle asked.

"Well…" She hesitated and turned her head to her brother. "Sure, we are flying by the seat of our pants!" Kate joked.

"No problem," Kyle said. "We're all cool, calm, and collected."

"Nothing's happening," Kate said.

"Flip the TT lever, and then adjust the time clock for the year 1490," Kyle said.

"Duh," Kate flicked the TT lever but mistakenly set the clock for 2490, because she was distracted by Will. She pulled back on the cyclic stick, shrieked, and pointed the chopper up toward Mars. The chopper shook and began to go vertical as the nose came up. Then the chopper rolled upside down into a continuous hyper-loop. They started accelerating into an energized loop when—*BAM*! Will slammed onto the windshield and looked like a frog clinging to it. But he was disguised as Harry with his face and clothes, so neither of the twins realized.They both shrieked! He pounded on the windshield until it cracked and then spider cracks developed throughout.

"Let me in!" he said. "Will is chasing me!"

"Oh my god!" Kyle yelled!" He reached around and unlocked the door.

Will flew around to the side of the helicopter and jerked open the door, and climbed into the back seat as the door slammed shut.

"Hi, kids, I have a surprise for you!" he said in Harry's voice. I'm not Harry but Will!"

The twins were scared. They stared straight ahead in disbelief. Will grabbed Kate by her ponytail and wadded his hand around it. He grabbed Kyle by his jacket collar and tugged till Kyle choked.

"Here's the deal, guys," Will said. "You help me kill Harry or I kill us all right now!"

"Kate struggled to speak. "We heard he might already be dead."

"Nope, but close. He is secured near the magnetic field in the UK. Once he wakes up, I need Kyle to lure him into the magnetic field while I hold onto you, Kate. No tricks, Kyle, because then your sister becomes my new girlfriend!"

"How do I know you will turn Kate loose after Harry is dead?" Kyle asked. "And why does he need to die?"

"Because he is a butthead and has ruined my plans to rule the adults."

"Why be such a *monster*?"

"I'm mad as heck and I hate adults that have been in my way all my life. And if you don't screw this up, I might put you in charge of one of my teams."

"Team of what—Bullies?" Kate said.

"Our goal is world dominance and to never let an adult boss kids around again. We are recruiting for bullies and think you two short little punks would be perfect spies to infiltrate schools and bring us kids to become bullies like us."

"Wow, you have taken being a bully to a new level," Kyle said. "Maybe you should grow up and get on with your life."

"Or maybe get an operation to fix the motherboard that is making you crazy!" Kate said.

"You just don't get it! How do I know if I'll wake up? I suggest you join us on our quest." Will tugged harder on Kate's hair and pulled tighter on Kyle's collar.

The twins were still frozen in their seats. The tail rotor glowed a-bright orange as the chopper reached maximum velocity. Within an instant, a gravity vortex was created and they were all swallowed into a black hole

Jon Wayne Faust is the author of two books with another two under development, *Helicopter Harry* and *Blondys Doggy Diary*. When he isn't writing he is photographing stunning landscapes, but his all-time favorite hobby is cycling. He has biked—toured four-thousand miles through New Zealand, Australia and Tasmania. And his adventurous spirit also took him to India for hip resurfacing surgery before he climbing Mount Kilimanjaro five months later on his 50th birthday.

CONNECT ONLINE

helicopterharry.com
jonwaynefaust.com